THIS SIGNED EDITION OF

I Have No Secrets

BY

Penny Joelson

HAS BEEN SPECIALLY BOUND BY THE PUBLISHER

LIMITED SIGNED EDITION FOR
TARGET BOOK CLUB

Dear Target Reader,

I was thrilled when I heard that *I Have No Secrets* had been chosen for the Target Book Club. I felt Jemma's joy too, as I know she'd be delighted that so many of you will have access to her story. That is how my main character, Jemma, feels to me—as if she is a real person, although she is, of course, entirely fictional. By the time you've finished reading the book, I hope that she will feel real to you, too, and that you will love her and connect with her as much as I do.

When I first had the idea for this story, I wanted to write a thriller in which the main character knew "who'd done it" but couldn't tell anyone for some reason. I didn't know what that reason would be, but then Jemma's character popped into my head—a teenage girl with severe cerebral palsy, unable to move or communicate. Although I have worked with people with disabilities, I still had some doubts. Could I do this?

Jemma's inner voice spoke to me and said, "Yes, you can! And you must!" Her voice in my head felt so strong, so powerful, so determined. Her character was already coming to life for me, and I couldn't say no. I had to write it. And as soon as I started, I felt that this book was going to be something special.

I was careful to get feedback from people with cerebral palsy—the most powerful note being from a young man who said he thought his parents, through reading my book, would understand better what it is like to be him. I was really moved by that.

We all need a voice, we all want to be heard, and we all know what it is like when people don't hear us. That's why I think Jemma's story is relevant to everyone.

Enjoy!

Penny Joelson

I HAVE NO SECRETS

I Have no Secrets

Penny Joelson

sourcebooks
fire

Published by Sourcebooks Fire, an imprint of Sourcebooks
P.O. Box 4410, Naperville, Illinois 60567-4410
(630) 961-3900
sourcebooks.com

Originally published in 2017 in Great Britain by Electric
Monkey, an imprint of Egmont UK, Ltd.

Library of Congress Cataloging-in-Publication Data

Names: Joelson, Penny, author.
Title: I have no secrets / Penny Joelson.
Description: Naperville, IL : Sourcebooks Fire, [2019] | "Originally published in
2017 in Great Britain by Electric Monkey, an imprint of Egmont UK, Ltd." |
Summary: Sixteen-year-old Jemma, who has severe cerebral palsy, must grapple
with dark truths that only she knows, and is unable to communicate.
Identifiers: LCCN 2019008889 | (trade pbk. : alk. paper)
Subjects: | CYAC: Secrets--Fiction. | Communication--Fiction. | Cerebral
palsy--Fiction. | People with disabilities--Fiction. | Foster children--Fiction.
Classification: LCC PZ7.1.J575 Iah 2019 | DDC [Fic]--dc23
LC record available at https://lccn.loc.gov/2019008889

Printed and bound in the United States of America.
WOZ 10 9 8 7 6 5 4 3 2 1

For Michael and Zoe

I HAVE NO SECRETS

1

I tense up as soon as I hear the doorbell. I know it's him. I know it's Dan. Sarah's still upstairs getting ready, and I hope she comes down soon. I don't want him coming in here.

Mom calls up to Sarah, and I hear Sarah say she'll be down in a minute. "We've been keeping her busy, I'm afraid," Mom tells Dan, "so she hasn't had much time to get ready!"

"I know she wouldn't have it any other way," says Dan. "She's a gem—and you too. What you do for these kids."

I listen to them chatting away and Mom laughing at Dan's jokes. Everyone loves Dan. Then Mom says she has to get back to the kitchen—she's left things on the stove and she's sure Sarah won't be long.

It's quiet for a moment. I hear the distant clattering of pans in the kitchen. Then I hear Dan's voice, coming closer as he speaks.

"What show are you watching? Ah...*Pointless!*"

I can hear him breathing. Then he whispers, "A little like your life, isn't it, Jemma?"

He's standing behind me now, but I can't see him because my wheelchair is facing the TV. I try to focus on the game show questions and forget he's there, but he gives a long, dramatic sigh.

"Don't know how you can stand it." His voice is low, not loud enough to be overheard. "Watching television must be the most excitement you get." He only speaks like this when no one else is around. He used to ignore me completely, but not anymore.

He moves so he is in front of me, blocking my view of the TV. Grimacing, he leans forward. I get a gulping feeling, a tightness in my throat.

"If I were you," he whispers, "I'd kill myself."

My heart thuds as he rubs his head, feigning thoughtfulness. "Oh, yeah... You can't, can you? Listen," he continues, "if you ever want a little help, I could—"

We both hear footsteps on the stairs. Dan backs away. His face transforms from ugly sneer to fake grin, his features softening as if they have been remolded.

"I'd have done better than that couple!" he says, laughing and pointing to the TV screen. "We should go on this show, shouldn't we, Sarah?"

I get a waft of Sarah's perfume, which is quickly overtaken by the smell of onions frying in the kitchen. "I'm useless at trivia," she says, laughing as she comes into view. "I bet Jemma could do it, though, if she had the chance."

I don't know about that, although I do sometimes get the right answers. It's possible I'd be better than Sarah. She's an awesome aide, but she's not too smart when it comes to general knowledge—or boyfriends.

Out of the corner of my eye, I see her kiss Dan softly on the lips.

My own mouth suddenly feels dry.

The couple playing *Pointless* have been eliminated. They look very disappointed. Dan and Sarah only have eyes for each other. "Ready?" Dan smiles at Sarah. "You look stunning, babe."

She nods and turns to me. Her eyes are sparkly, her cheeks flushed. "Bye, Jem. See you in the morning."

"See you, Jemma," says Dan. He winks at me.

2

"Sorry to leave you so long, dear!"

Mom bustles into the room, and I'm relieved to hear her warm, soft voice. She switches off the TV and pushes my wheelchair into the kitchen, to my place at the end of the table.

I hear the car in the drive. Dad's back from taking Finn to his swimming lesson and picking up Olivia from ballet. Soon the kitchen is noisy and cheerful, as usual, and I push Dan out of my mind.

Olivia is boasting to Mom about how good her dancing was, and I watch as she shows Mom the new steps while Mom tries to get her to sit down at the table. She's nine and has only been here a year. We're all fostered. I've been here since I was two and so has Finn, who's nearly six. I've heard Mom say Olivia was "hard to place." Maybe that goes for Finn and me too, though Olivia's problems are different from ours. Finn is autistic, and right now, he is lining all his beans up neatly on the plate with his fingers. He's obsessed with straight lines.

Olivia is a whirlwind—sometimes a tornado—and she's loud. Finn and I don't speak, so life is very different and much noisier since she came.

"Sit down, Olivia!" Dad says in his "firm but kind" voice, and Olivia finally does. At least she doesn't start one of her tantrums.

Mom serves Dad's lasagna, then starts feeding me my mushed-up version. Dan's words creep back into my head while I'm eating, and I try to shut them out.

"If I were you, I'd kill myself. Listen, if you ever want a little help, I could—"

I can't believe he said it—as if my life is worth nothing!

Olivia is wolfing down her food like she's never eaten before. She's skinny, but she has a huge appetite. Finn isn't eating. He's still lining up his beans, concentrating as if his life depends on it.

"Come on, Finn," Dad coaxes. "Time to eat them now."

But Finn clearly doesn't think his line is straight enough.

"Finn, my love," says Mom gently, "why don't you start with the lasagna?"

I don't think Finn is listening to Mom, but I think he's happy now with his line of beans. In any event, he forks a small amount of lasagna into his mouth.

Mom spoons some more into mine.

"I saw Paula earlier," she tells Dad. "She looks dreadful, the poor woman."

"Still no news?" Dad asks. Mom shakes her head.

"News about what?" Olivia demands.

Paula lives down the street, and her son, Ryan, was murdered last month. He was nineteen, and he was stabbed to death, and no one knows who did it. Everyone's talking about it, though—it's even been on the radio.

Dad quickly changes the subject.

"Finn's swimming like a fish now," he tells Mom. "He's come along so fast."

"And I was really good at ballet!" Olivia says, never wanting to be left out.

"I'm sure you were," says Dad.

"How was school?" Mom asks Olivia. She shrugs.

Olivia never wants to talk about school. It's like it's some big secret for her.

I have no secrets of my own. I've never done anything without someone knowing about it. I'm sixteen years old, and I have severe cerebral palsy. I am quadriplegic, which means I can't control my arms or legs—or anything else. I can't eat by myself. I can't go to the bathroom without help. I can't move without someone lifting me with a hoist or pushing me in a wheelchair. I also can't speak.

I've been this way all my life. I can see, though, and I can hear. Sometimes people forget that; they don't realize that I have a functioning brain. Sometimes people talk about me as if I'm not even there. I hate that.

And sometimes people tell me their secrets. I think it's because it's really hard to hold a one-way conversation. If they are alone with me, they want to talk to pass the time and they end up telling me stuff. They know I won't tell anyone else, so they think telling me is safe. The perfect listener.

Sarah told me her secret. She's cheating on Dan. She's still seeing Richard, her old boyfriend, because he's so sweet and she can't stand to hurt him by breaking up with him. Neither of them knows the other exists. I'm always worried when Sarah has a boyfriend, although I enjoy the way she gossips to me about them. She has this dream of a fairy-tale wedding—she's even shown me pictures of her ideal wedding dress online. I know I should want her to be happy, and I do. It's just that I'd miss her so much if she went off to get married. She's the best aide I've had.

More than that, I don't want her to marry someone who isn't good enough for her. And I definitely don't want her marrying Dan.

3

Sarah's in a great mood when she's back on duty the next morning, though I can tell she has a hangover and is trying to hide it. She's drinking a lot of coffee. She clearly had a good night out with Dan and is singing a track by our favorite band, Glowlight.

She's wheeling me from my bedroom to the kitchen when I hear the clunk of mail landing on the mat. Sarah stops to pick it up and puts the small pile of letters on the kitchen table.

"Oh, look—one for you, Jemma," she comments. As she pushes me into my place, I see that the top letter, though addressed to Mom and Dad, has my name on it too—*Parents/Guardians of Jemma Shaw*. I rarely get mail. I wonder what it could be.

Mom picks up the pile and glances down. Then she quickly moves my letter to the bottom and puts them all on the kitchen counter. Sarah doesn't seem to notice.

Now I am even more curious. Why doesn't Mom want to open it?

After breakfast, Sarah goes to get Olivia ready, and Dad gets up to leave for work. Mom follows him out into the hallway to kiss him goodbye. Their voices are muffled, but I can pick out Mom's words. She says, "There's been another letter. I haven't read it yet, but I think we'll have to tell her."

I strain to hear Dad's reply. "Yes—she is family. Jemma has a right to know."

Family? What are they talking about? If only I could ask. It sounds like they're planning to tell me. I just have to hope that they do.

Dad's gone and Sarah's in the kitchen with me, easing my arms gently into my coat, ready for school. I'm conscious that my letter is still there, at the bottom of the pile on the counter.

Olivia's moaning that she can't find her reading book.

Mom sighs. "When did you last have it, Olivia?"

Olivia shrugs. "Dunno."

"Take a look in your bedroom," Mom tells her.

Olivia heads off slowly toward the stairs.

"Sarah, can you go with her?" Mom asks. "I don't see her book down here."

"Sure," says Sarah. "You're ready, Jemma. That's one down at least!" She hurries off after Olivia.

"Where's Finn's water bottle?" Mom mutters to herself. "I'm sure I washed it yesterday. I bet you know where I put it, Jemma."

As it happens, I do know. I saw it fall off the dish rack and down behind the trash can.

The doorbell rings, and Mom wheels me toward the door. We never know if my minibus or Finn's cab will come first. Today, it's the cab that takes Finn to his special school.

Mom sighs and pushes a spare green water bottle into Finn's bag, which is not going to please Finn, because he always has the blue one. She helps him with his coat and gives his hair a quick comb. He wriggles away as fast as he can and out the front door with his taxi escort, Jo.

"Reading book found," Sarah says, coming down the stairs.

"I hope you said thank you, Olivia," says Mom, though she knows full well that Olivia hasn't.

"It wasn't me who lost it, Lorraine!" Olivia protests. "Why do you always blame me? It's not my fault!"

She stamps her feet, and I'm relieved when the doorbell rings again so I can leave before Olivia starts screaming.

But all I think about as the bus proceeds down the street is the letter. I try to figure out what Mom and Dad were talking about. Family? Mom has an aunt and Dad has a brother, but we don't see much of them because they live a long way from here. Were they talking about their family? Or could it be *mine*—like my birth mom, the one who gave birth to me and then dumped me? Could she have finally decided she wants to see me?

I hope it's not her. I don't want to see her—not ever! She probably only wants to get a look at me and stare. I hope Mom and Dad tell her to get lost.

As soon as Dad is back in the evening, I start waiting for them to talk to me—but they don't say anything. I couldn't even see my letter in the kitchen at dinnertime. The whole pile was gone. Have they changed their minds, or are they waiting for Finn and Olivia to be in bed so they can talk about it? I'm not exactly looking forward to a conversation about my birth mom, but waiting for it is even worse.

Dad does the dishes while Mom and Sarah put Finn and Olivia to bed. It seems like it takes forever, even though I know it is probably just the normal amount of time. But then, finally, when it's nearly my bedtime and I'm watching TV on my own, Mom and Dad both come in. Mom pauses the TV, and Dad turns me around to face the sofa and sits down, looking serious.

He has the letter in his hand. I get a surge of relief mixed with panic.

"We've got something to tell you, Jemma," he says gently. "Something important."

My heart is beating so fast. Suddenly I don't want to hear—I don't want to know.

"We've gotten a letter," Dad continues, "from Social Services." He pauses, as if unsure how to continue.

Mom sits down beside him. "Jemma, I know this is going

to be a bit of a shock, and I will explain why we haven't told you before…"

I wait.

Dad reaches out and touches my hand. "You've got a sister, Jemma."

What?

A sister?

Mom sighs and smiles. "Her name's Jodi."

I try to take it in. The shock is making me breathless. A *sister*. I was so sure it was my birth mom wanting to see me. A sister is something completely different.

"The thing is," Mom continues, "we knew she wasn't told about you. So we thought it might be upsetting for you to know about her. But she found your name mentioned in some papers, and… I'm sorry, Jemma. It's been hard to know what to do."

They knew! All this time Mom and Dad have known that I have a sister. So many feelings are swirling around inside me. The thought of them not telling me makes me angry—but Mom's right. It would have been hard knowing about my sister if she was never going to know about me. I am still in shock, but I'm curious too.

A sister. My sister. I start to wonder what she's like—how old she is…

"The papers Jodi found were her adoption papers," Mom continues. "You and Jodi were split up when you were put into foster care. Your birth mom couldn't cope. She had a lot of problems. She was very young and on her own."

I've sometimes imagined it—my mom giving me up. I could even picture her face, horrified at her own baby, unable to deal with what I was. But there were two of us, two children. That idea had never entered my head. And she couldn't look after my sister either. Does my sister have a disability too? I'm not sure what to make of this—but I know it changes things. It changes everything.

"Jodi's been asking if she can contact you," says Dad, drawing me out of my thoughts.

I get a surge of excitement that quickly sinks when I think what they would have had to tell Jodi—that I can't exactly contact her back.

"She's been persistent, but we weren't sure if it was a good idea," says Mom. "It's so hard when you can't tell us how you feel about it... But we've told her about you, and we've said she can write to you. I hope it's what you want, Jemma. I really do."

My sister! I'm still finding it hard to believe that I have one. I wonder how much she's been told about me. Will she really want to know me once she finds out what I'm like? I am thrilled, though. I can't wait to know more about her. She's going to write to me! My sister is going to write to me!

4

"I still can't believe you've got a sister and no one told you!" Sarah exclaims, as she picks up a book to read to me in bed. "I knew nothing, Jemma. Your mom and dad never even mentioned her."

I definitely believe her—if Mom and Dad had told Sarah about Jodi, she would have let something slip. She'd never keep something like that from me.

"Me and my sister, Kate," says Sarah, "we don't always get along, but I can't imagine growing up and not knowing her. I bet you can't wait for a letter from Jodi!"

Sarah keeps mentioning Jodi over the next couple of days. It's as if she's as excited as I am. I wish I could tell her how nervous it makes me. What if Jodi doesn't write?

At least it means Sarah's not talking about Dan so much. I can almost start to pretend he doesn't exist. In fact, today Sarah isn't talking at all—she's concentrating as she battles to get my rebellious arms into the sleeves of a sweater. My muscle spasms are worse than usual because I haven't been sleeping well. Thinking about my sister has kept me awake. "Tonight's the night," she whispers. I wonder what she means. She's not seeing Dan again, is she? She's seeing so much of him that I'm sometimes scared she's going to run off with him! But of course, she'd never do that.

"I'm breaking up with Richard," she says. "It has to be done. I'm not being fair to him." She runs a brush quickly but gently through my tangled hair. "I can't keep putting it off. I know he'll be heartbroken, though—he's such a softy."

At last Sarah is doing the right thing. It's no good going out with someone just because you feel sorry for them. Now she just needs to dump Dan too! I wish she had more sense when it comes to men. She's had a few boyfriends since she's been here, and they've all been hopeless. Like Jason, who was always borrowing money from her and never paying it back, and a guy named Mario who was only interested in football and a total bore. Next was wimpy Richard. And then Dan came along.

Sarah's in her room getting ready to go out when the doorbell rings. She's meeting Richard downtown, so I know it's not him. I'm in the living room, but the door's open and for once I'm at an angle where I can see into the hall. Dad opens the front door. I hear Dan's voice greeting him.

What's *he* doing here? Sarah is definitely not expecting him.

Dad invites Dan in. I hear the front door shut, then watch them as they talk about the weather. When Dan sees Sarah all dressed up, what's he going to think? He'll get suspicious for sure. I strain to listen, but now Olivia has started one of her tantrums. She's lying on the floor somewhere behind me, kicking and screaming like a two-year-old except twice as loud.

I hear Dad call upstairs, "Sarah! Dan's here!"

He's assumed Sarah is going out with Dan tonight! At least he's warned her. It would be awful if she came down and just found Dan in the hall. I have no idea what she's going to do.

Thankfully, Dan doesn't come into the living room. I think Olivia's screaming is keeping him at a distance. Mom comes to see what's up with her, saying a quick hello to Dan as she passes. She turns my wheelchair around, which is annoying because I'd rather watch what's happening in the hall than look at Olivia, who is lying on the floor at the far end of the room, pointing and screaming. Now I can see what's upset her. One of her ballet shoes is trapped on the candelabra light fixture, near the ceiling. Finn must have thrown it up there. He's got good aim.

Mom calms Olivia and says Dad will get it down. Finn is nowhere to be seen. Mom turns me to face the TV and switches it on. Then she pulls Olivia up gently, hugging her, and holds her hand to lead her out. I hear them going upstairs.

I'm conscious that Dan is still in the hall. Sarah calls to say she'll be down in a few minutes. Then I hear Dan sigh. He walks into the room and goes straight to the TV and picks up the remote, flicking through channels. He's acting as if I'm not even here. I wish I could say, "Hey! I was watching that!" even though I wasn't really.

He settles on the news. I don't want the news. On the screen I can see a casket being carried into a church. A reporter is speaking. It's only when I hear him say the name Ryan Blake that I start paying attention.

Ryan—from down the street. It was his funeral today. I want to know what the police have found out. Mom and Dad think Ryan might have been into drugs. "Police are still seeking witnesses," the reporter continues, "and his parents are pleading for anyone who knows anything to come forward." Dan suddenly turns toward me.

"You don't know anything, do you, Jem?" he sniggers.

I can't stand it when he calls me "Jem," as if he's part of the family or something.

"Here's a secret for you," he continues, "and I know you won't tell anyone." He winks. There's a pause. He presses his face close to mine, so close I can feel his hot breath on my cheeks. "They're never gonna catch me!" he whispers, squinting his eyes and then nodding at the screen. He stands back, smiling, as if he's gloating. "There's something for you to chew on, *freak*!"

Sarah's feet patter on the stairs.

Dan quickly changes the channel to a game show. *Catch him? What did he mean?* It's an attempt to irritate me—it must be...

"Hiya, babe," he says.

"What are you doing here?" Sarah asks. I see her flapping her arms a little, like Finn does. I can tell she's panicking, but she's also gazing longingly into Dan's eyes. She won't cancel on Richard to go out with Dan, will she? She needs to break up with *both* of them. I wish she could hear what I'm telling her in my head.

"You left a glove in my car," he tells her. "I just found it today. I was passing by, so I thought I'd drop it off. Don't want you getting chilly fingers!"

"Oh, thanks! I was wondering where it was," she replies. "But I've got to get going. I'm headed out with Emma and Rihanna. We're going to the movies."

"Out again?" he says.

"Yes, I switched my next night off. It's Emma's birthday," Sarah says quickly. Sarah seems to have her excuse ready— but I guess this is what she's told Mom. "We're having a girls' night out. Becks is coming too. We're seeing that movie you said was for lovestruck teenage girls."

"No way!"

"Yeah, really." Sarah laughs for a little too long. "And I've gotta go or I'll be late."

"No worries, I'll give you a lift," says Dan.

"No, Dan. I'm fine," Sarah assures him.

"It's no prob," says Dan.

"Oh... All right," she replies.

An uneasy feeling grips my chest. I don't want her to go with him. What he said to me... He had to be joking. Dan's horrible, but he wouldn't actually kill someone. Would he? And why did he turn up here this evening? It doesn't feel right. Maybe she's done something to make him suspicious. Was he trying to catch her at it?

Sarah says goodbye to me and touches my hand gently. Her hand is hot. She knows this is a mess, and she briefly meets my eyes with a look that says she knows I know this too. She turns to the door.

"Bye, Jemma," Dan says, winking again. I see his sneering face in my head when he called me *freak* and remember what else he said. I don't trust him one little bit.

They go, and I hear the front door bang shut.

Dad comes in and stares up at the ballet shoe on the light fixture, muttering, "You've got to be joking," under his breath.

5

Mom gets me ready for bed, but I'm barely listening as she chats away about needing to get me some new clothes. What did Dan mean?

If only Mom could see inside my head to the thoughts spinning around. But I know on the outside I must look exactly the same as I always do. Nothing shows. No one knows.

He must have been joking. If he was involved, wouldn't we have heard something? Wouldn't he be a suspect? Even so, I wish I could tell someone. Just so they know what he's like. Just in case.

If he was confessing, he knew he was telling the one person who would keep his secret safe. Maybe he thinks I don't even understand what he says. I just want to know for sure. Because if Dan is a murderer, and he finds out Sarah is cheating on him...

I can't sleep at all, waiting to know that Sarah is back home. My room is downstairs, but at the back of the house, and I listen for the sound of the front door. Finally I hear her come in, but I'm facing away from my bedside clock so I can't see the time. Maybe she'll come in to turn me—I have to be turned in the night so I don't get sore from being in one position. Yes. I can hear her footsteps.

She's breathing quite fast, and her hands aren't as gentle as usual. She catches my eye in the dimmed light and sees that I'm awake. I will her to tell me what happened. Sometimes Sarah seems to read my mind. That's one of the things I love about her.

"That wasn't the best evening of my life," she whispers.

I wait eagerly for more. She sits down on the edge of the bed.

"I can't believe Dan turned up! That glove thing was just an excuse, don't you think? He's getting so serious. He said he couldn't bear to be apart from me." She laughs. "I sat in his car with my fingers crossed that he wouldn't think something was wrong. Then he wanted to actually come into the theater with me, but luckily it was really hard to park so he couldn't."

She runs her hand through her hair. Only Sarah would get herself into this situation.

"I was scared he might hang around so I texted Richard from the lobby to say I'd be late and waited ten minutes before I even dared walk to the bar! You've gotta laugh, Jem."

Sarah is not taking this seriously at all. At least it sounds like Dan didn't catch her.

"When I got there," she continues, "Richard looked so pleased to see me. I just couldn't do it to him."

My heart sinks. Sarah is fidgeting and looks excited about something. Has she changed her mind and decided she wants to be with Richard after all?

"Jem, he got tickets for us to see Glowlight next month! It'll be amazing!" She gives me a sheepish look. "Is it really bad if I keep going out with him until then?"

Glowlight! Well, it's not great to use him for his tickets, but it is Glowlight. Maybe I'd do the same... No, this is wrong. Sarah needs to break up with Richard!

"Perhaps we could just go to the concert as friends," she continues. "But I don't think Richard would like that. I know Dan wouldn't."

She sighs and smooths my comforter down. "I'm such a coward, Jem."

I don't know what I'd do if I were Sarah—though I'd like to think I wouldn't get myself into such a mess in the first place.

6

When the bus drops me off from school on Monday, Mom tells me we have visitors. She pushes my wheelchair into the kitchen, where Mr. and Mrs. Blake are drinking tea. Paula and Mom have known each other for years, but more to say hello in the street than as actual friends. I remember her coming to Mom a few times when Ryan was young and acting up, asking Mom for advice. I think there was a time when she even hoped Mom would foster him.

Since Ryan died, Mom has tried to be supportive, and Paula's been here a few times. Graham—Mr. Blake—doesn't usually come with her, though.

Paula says hi to me and smiles, but her grief is clear in the deep lines on her face and her drooping eyes. Graham shifts awkwardly and taps the rim of his mug with his finger. I can tell that I make him uncomfortable. I notice he's kept his black outdoor jacket on, while Paula has taken off her coat.

He's clearly hoping not to be here long.

"I know he was no angel," Paula is saying to Mom, "but I was so hard on him—always nagging, criticizing, pushing him to change. The last thing I said to him was, 'Get out and don't come back!' Can you believe it? That's what I said!"

She bursts into tears.

Graham touches her shoulder and fidgets again.

Mom hands Paula a tissue.

"I know," says Mom, "but you could never have known what would happen. You were trying to set boundaries. He knew you loved him. He knew that's why you kept after him."

"Do you really think so?" Paula sobs.

When we were young, Ryan used to stick his tongue out at me if he passed me in the street. Then when he got a little older, he called me "Spaz" or "Spazzie" or worse things. He even spat at me once.

I don't miss Ryan, but obviously I feel horrible for Paula. Ryan was a loser, but he was still her son—and Graham's.

I look at Graham. He's like a block of stone. Paula sips her tea. "I can't bear the thought that the monster who did it is walking around free. I might pass him in the street and never know."

Dan's face comes into my mind. *Yes, you might*, I think. *He was here... He was here in this house*, I want to tell Paula. A sound comes out of my mouth, a strained gurgle. Paula glances at me and quickly away again.

I wish I could tell them what he said. Just in case. I don't know if Dan and Ryan even knew each other. They were very different. And Dan doesn't seem like he'd be involved with drugs and gangs and stuff. Or maybe he's just good at hiding it.

"We'd better be going," Graham says gruffly.

Paula turns and gives him a bewildered look. But she pulls herself up from the chair, and Graham helps her put her coat on.

"At least the *Crime Watch* thing might help," I hear Mom say as they go to the front door. "Let's just hope someone calls in and the police get a lead."

So Ryan's murder is going to be on *Crime Watch Daily*! Maybe that will make everything clear. I hope Mom and Dad will let me watch it. I've never seen it, but I know about it—how they reconstruct crimes, and people watching can phone in if they know anything. Maybe there will be a clue that will tell me if Dan really did it—and if he did, then Sarah or Mom or Dad or someone else watching will have to realize it was him.

On Tuesday after school, Sarah greets me with a smile even bigger than her usual cheerful one.

"Ooh, Jem! A letter's come from your sister! Your mom hasn't opened it. She's waiting for you. But I hope she'll show me later! I'm dying to know what your sister said."

Sarah wheels me into the kitchen, announcing, "Jemma's home!" to Mom. She doesn't leave. I think she's hoping Mom will let her stay.

"Thanks, Sarah," says Mom.

Sarah shoots me a pretend annoyed look and goes, closing the door behind her. We sit at the kitchen table, and Mom carefully opens the white envelope.

My heart thuds.

"Are you ready for this?" Mom asks. She puts the letter down so I can see it.

"*Dear Jemma,*" she reads.

I didn't know you existed until a few months ago. I found some papers in a drawer that were about me. One of them had your name on it under mine. My name is Jodi, and I am your sister!

Mom pauses and looks up at me before continuing.

In fact, more than that, Jemma. We are twins!

Twins? Mom never told me that.

We must have been born only minutes apart. The thing is, I've always had this weird feeling—like something was missing. When I found out about you I thought, This is it! This explains it. I have a twin sister. We spent nine months together before we were born, and we've been separated ever since.

Missing? I've never felt that. But maybe that's because so much else is missing for me—like legs and arms that work and a voice.

Mom is still reading.

Now I'm going to tell you some stuff about me. I live in Enfield—only a few miles from you! I live with my mom and dad (the ones who adopted me), but I don't

have any brothers or sisters. I've ALWAYS wanted
a sister.

Favorite things. Color—purple. Food—ice-cream
sundae. Sport—field hockey (I play for the school team).
Pet—cat (Mine's called Fluff. She really is like a fluffy
white bundle, and I love her to pieces! She disappeared
last year and was found up in a tree after three days!).
People—my best friend, Ava, my boyfriend, Jack, and
my parents too. They are terrific, and even though I was
angry that they didn't tell me about you and they were
upset that I found out, they've calmed down now and say
they're sorry that they didn't tell me before.

There's so much more I could write, but I'll stop now
because I've got tons of homework.

I know you have disabilities and that you can't
write back. I've been told about that. It's no big deal.
Don't worry, I'll keep writing!

I've put in a photo of me, though our printer at home
is worthless and it came out a little dark. I'll try to find
a better photo—and maybe next time I'll send you a
picture of Fluff too!

I will write again soon.

Love, Jodi

Mom holds the photo so I can see it. It's kind of blurry,

but Jodi has dark hair like mine, and her eyes are a little like mine too. She looks pretty.

"I'll reply for you, Jemma," says Mom. "And I'll encourage Jodi to keep writing. We'll take things slowly, and hopefully one day you'll be able to meet her."

I'm only half listening. I can't take my eyes off the photo. That's my sister—my twin sister!

Mom puts the photo by my bed, and looking at it and thinking about the letter keeps me happy for the next couple of days. I am sleeping better too. It is almost enough to keep me from thinking about Dan. But when Thursday evening comes, I am desperate for Dad to let me stay in the living room to watch *Crime Watch*.

Sarah's upstairs putting Finn and Olivia to bed, and Mom's getting her coat on to go to Weight Watchers. She's been trying to eat healthily, but I know her secret—I see her hide chocolate bars between the books on the highest shelf in the living room.

I'm hoping my limbs stay still and no sounds escape my mouth so she'll forget I'm here. Dad is more likely to let me watch *Crime Watch* than Mom. But she comes to say goodbye to me and then turns to Dad.

"I'm not sure Jemma should see it," she says. "It might upset her."

"She's sixteen," says Dad. "I bet she'd be interested to see it, wouldn't you, Jemma?" He turns to me and back to Mom. "It's not as if she hasn't heard us all talk about it."

I wish I could hug Dad.

Mom still looks uncertain. She glances from Dad to me and back again.

Please!

"All right," says Mom. "Hopefully I'll be back in time, but if not, you'll have to fill me in."

When the show starts, I'm disappointed that Sarah isn't here—but Dad calls her, and she brings a basket of laundry to fold and sits on the armchair.

Mom gets back just as they start showing Ryan's case and hurries in, still in her coat.

"Put on two pounds." She sighs, and I hear the sofa creak as she sits down next to Dad.

"Four weeks ago," the reporter says, "nineteen-year-old Ryan Blake was brutally stabbed to death in Walden Cross. The assailant and motive remain a mystery. Witnesses have helped to make the reenactment that you are about to see."

They show actors, including one I can clearly see is meant to be Ryan, drinking in a local bar, the Hare and Hound. Then Ryan and his friends leave and gradually split up until Ryan is left with one friend, who finally heads for home. Instead of going home himself, Ryan doubles back. No one knows why he did this. He heads down a side street—though they're not sure which one—and comes out somewhere behind the train station.

That was where his body was found.

"Did you see Ryan on Warduff Street or Mackenzie Avenue between 11:00 p.m. and midnight?" the reporter asks. "A man in a black jacket was seen walking along Mackenzie Avenue just before 11:00. This man has not yet been identified. Are you that man, or did you also see him that night?"

I try to think like Hercule Poirot. I've listened to dozens of Agatha Christie audiobooks that Mom's aunt gave me. I need to be observant—to have an eye for anything that might be a clue, even if it seems unlikely. Everyone is a suspect in Agatha Christie. Ryan's friends seem like a shady bunch. Maybe the last friend he was with didn't go home. Maybe he doubled back too. Perhaps Ryan had lied to him—or one of the others—or ripped them off. But there isn't much to go on to figure out a motive. What about the man in the black jacket? Dan has a black jacket, but it's a little different from the one they showed.

Suddenly I remember Graham—Ryan's dad—sitting in our kitchen. His jacket looked like the one on the program. Graham? Is it possible? Could he have gotten so fed up with Ryan that he lost his temper and killed him? One of the crime books I listened to said most people are killed by members of their families. And in Agatha Christie it's often the quiet ones you have to watch. But Graham? Murder his own son?

It's easier to believe that Dan did it. I've seen what he can be like—even though no one else has.

I want to see Sarah's reaction, but I'm facing the TV. I wish she'd say something.

"Police say the alley behind the station is known to be used by drug dealers," the reporter continues, "but no drugs were found in Ryan's blood." They mention that the knife used hasn't been found, and they give the number for people to call.

"Okay, Jemma," says Mom. For a moment I imagine her dialing the number and handing me the phone so I can tell them what Dan said. But of course, she's just telling me that it's time for me to go to bed.

Sarah wheels me out as *Crime Watch* moves on to a series of armed robberies in Dartford.

"Listen, dear, I've got something to tell you," Mom says the next evening.

I'm all ears—wondering if it's to do with *Crime Watch*. No one's mentioned it since yesterday, and I've been waiting for news. Did anyone call the program? Do the police have any new leads?

Then I wonder if it's Jodi. Has she written again? "You remember I told you about Carlstone College?" Mom says. "I've arranged for us to go up there next week."

My mind whirls because this is so far from what I was thinking about. *Carlstone College.* When Mom talked about it before, she said I might go there when I'm older—not *now*. Has she changed her mind?

"They have a communications expert coming," Mom tells me. "Professor Spalding. It's a meeting for any interested families, even those whose children aren't at the college. I can't make any promises, but maybe he'll be able to help you.

And we can have a look around, just to see what the college is like."

A while ago, they showed me a leaflet for Carlstone. Mom said they had amazing facilities and might be able to help me much more than the school I'm at. I liked the sound of the college. I thought I might really enjoy it, and they offer many more subjects there. Then Mom told me it's a three-hour drive from here. I'd have to live there, like at a boarding school.

Mom said if I went there, she and Dad would come and visit, and I'd be able to come home some weekends and for school vacations. I was so relieved the next day when Mom said she thought I was too young, and maybe some time in the future we'd all go and have a look at it. But I thought that meant in a couple of years—not a couple of months.

And what about Sarah? If she went with me, it wouldn't be so bad, but I bet students don't get to take their own care-givers. And she wouldn't want to be three hours away from Dan, would she?

I try to focus on what Mom is saying about the communications expert. Hopefully, our visit really is just about seeing this professor. But I can't stop thinking that it might be something more. The worry is gnawing at my brain, joining the other worries and the questions I can never ask.

I feel myself withdrawing like a turtle into a shell. Mom's still talking, but I'm no longer listening.

When Sarah comes to fetch me for dinner, she looks at me for a moment and frowns. "What's up, Jem?"

I don't know how she can tell that something's wrong, but she can and I'm glad. Maybe my limbs are even stiffer than usual when she moves me. I certainly feel stiffer. Everything aches.

"I hope you're not coming down with something," she continues.

She looks into my eyes for clues. I wish they could give her some. She feels my forehead and inspects my arms, legs, and chest for rashes. Then she gets the ear thermometer and takes my temperature. Hopefully once she's figured out I'm not sick, she'll realize how unhappy I am.

Sarah wheels me into the kitchen. Everyone else is already at the table, but the silverware is missing. Finn has removed it and lined it all up neatly on the floor against the wall—a row of forks, then knives, then spoons.

Dad shakes his head at Finn and sighs as he picks them up, and there is a delay while he washes them in the sink. He isn't angry. He understands Finn.

"Something's wrong with Jemma," Sarah tells Mom. I watch Mom's face. Will she make the connection and realize that what she said before has made me worry?

"Are you hungry?" Mom asks me. "Sorry dinner's a little late."

I'm not hungry. And now I feel sick at the thought of eating.

Sarah shakes her head. "It's more than that."

Mom shrugs rather dismissively, and then I wonder if maybe she doesn't want Sarah to know about her plans, because Sarah will lose her job if I'm sent away. Once the silverware is washed and dried, Sarah spoons food into my mouth. I find it hard to swallow. Olivia knocks her cup over. I'm not sure if it is accidental or on purpose, but water spreads in a pool across the table and Dad's "Oh, Olivia" is enough to start her wailing theatrically. Dad tells her to calm down, which brings on a full-blown tantrum. My head is pounding now.

Mom and Dad are both fussing over Olivia. I scream inside my head sometimes, making the kind of noise she's making now, but of course no one ever knows.

Sarah aims another spoonful into my mouth. I cough and splutter. I can't stop coughing. I need a drink. Sarah is distracted, looking at Olivia, and I start to panic. I feel like I can't breathe. It is a moment before she sits me forward in my wheelchair and pats me on the back. She holds the straw to my lips and looks from me to Mom as Olivia finally stops shrieking. "I told you something was wrong. I think she's coming down with something. I'll sleep in her room tonight."

No one understands. When I'm worried and I just want reassurance, I have no way of getting it. Then my worries just grow and grow. Mom and Dad assume it's something physical because it so often is, but all I want is to be able to tell them how I feel.

"Thanks, Sarah," says Mom. "There's a nasty flu bug going around. I hope it isn't that."

Later, Sarah is getting me ready for bed when her cell phone rings.

"It's Dan. We haven't spoken all week. I'd better answer," she says apologetically, "or he might think I'm avoiding him."

She says hello and then puts the phone on speaker and leaves it on the bed while she crouches to take off my socks. I hear Dan's voice as clearly as if he's in the room.

"How was the movie, babe?"

Sarah has taken off one of my socks and started on the other one. She stops, bites her lip, and leans toward the phone. "Great," she chirps.

"Really? What was so great about it?" he asks.

"Why do you care?" Sarah asks. "It's not your kind of movie. You said so yourself."

"Just asking," he says.

There's a pause. "Sorry," says Sarah, "I can't talk now. I'm getting Jemma ready for bed. She's not feeling well. I'll call you later and tell you all about it, okay?"

"Sure—talk later. Love you, babe!"

Sarah puts her phone in her pocket, then laughs. "I'll have to look up some reviews online," she tells me. "I don't even know who's in it!"

9

"Come on, Finn!" Mom calls cheerfully as we reach the gate of the park.

When I woke up this morning, I had this weird floaty feeling, as if nothing in my life is real. I am apparently neither sick nor well. It doesn't surprise me that my body's behaving weirdly. All these thoughts have got to get out somehow. Sarah and Mom keep taking my temperature. "A little under the weather" is how Mom described me. We often go to the park on Saturdays, and she said some fresh air might do me good.

"We'll go and see the ducks first," Mom tells Finn and Olivia.

If I could roll my eyes, I would. I liked being taken to see the ducks when I was six, but right now I've got other things on my mind. If we have to be here, I was hoping we were going to the park café. It's at the top of the hill, and I know it's not easy to push me up there, but from the top you get a view right over the park. I like the feeling of being so high—on top of the world, looking down. From my wheelchair I so often feel low down, looking up at things.

Olivia skips ahead, Sarah's pushing me, and Mom's cajoling Finn—who is walking slowly, flapping his hand in front of his face. I think he likes the patterns of light it makes. Soon we reach the pond, and we stop by the barrier, near a clump of early daffodils. I watch Olivia throw corn at the nearest ducks as if she's trying to murder one. I'm sure she just said, "Yeah! Got it!"

Mom pushes corn into Finn's hand and helps him aim, but the corn just drops onto the sidewalk. He isn't really interested and starts to pull away toward the playground.

"OK, Finn, just a minute," Mom tells him.

Sarah's phone beeps. I bet it's Dan texting her. I see her peering at it when Mom's not looking. I wish she'd tell me what he said.

When we're in the playground, Sarah wheels me onto the wheelchair-accessible merry-go-round and pushes the bar gently so the platform begins to move before she gets on and stands with me.

"Just a gentle spin today, okay?"

This merry-go-round is here because of my mom; she campaigned for it for years, and I was so happy when it arrived. I used to like going fast. It's not often I get to do anything fast. I'm too old for it now, though, and especially not today when my head is already spinning. At least Sarah moves it slowly.

"I'll push!" Olivia says, running up.

"Gently, Olivia," Sarah tells her. But she's pushing too fast so I'm whirling even faster than the thoughts in my head. I want to stop. I want to get off. Now.

"Olivia! Slow down!" Sarah yells. She leaps off and brings it to a halt.

Olivia rushes away toward the playground climbers. "Sorry, Jemma! Are you okay?" Sarah asks, touching my shoulder as she pulls the wheelchair off the merry-go-round. I feel giddy and breathless. I want to go home. Sarah's phone beeps with another message.

She parks me next to a bench where we can watch Finn on the swing. She turns me carefully to make sure the low sun isn't in my eyes. The swing squeaks noisily. Finn would happily swing for an hour, maybe two, if he were allowed.

Sarah takes out her phone again and reads the new message. I wonder if she managed to convince Dan that she really went to the movies.

Olivia runs around, going on everything. She demands that Mom watch her on the monkey bars and then on the climbing wall. She's good at climbing as well as dancing.

I might definitely be too old for playgrounds, but I'd rather be here, with Mom and Sarah and Olivia and Finn, than packed off to some college.

I'm wrapped well in a warm coat and have a blanket over my knees, but I'm starting to feel cold. The fresh air is doing me no good at all, which is no surprise to me. I feel weak and fuzzy-headed. The squeaking of the swing is hurting my ears.

Sarah looks up from her phone. "You're very pale, Jemma."

She goes over to Mom and asks if she can take me home.

Mom comes and looks at me and nods at Sarah. "Yes, you guys go. We won't be far behind."

Sarah pushes me along the sidewalk, past the local stores, the newsstand, and the barbershop.

"Oh, look! See that man coming out of Off-Track Betting?" says Sarah. "I know him—it's Billy."

"Hi, Billy!" Sarah calls as the man walks toward us. He has his head down, but his shoulders jolt and he looks up sharply, then stops and smiles at her.

"Sarah!" he says. "You all right?"

Sarah has mentioned Billy. He's a friend of Dan's. She said Dan calls him "Billy No Brains," which sounded mean to me. Sarah just thought it was funny. My head's really aching now. I hope she's not going to talk for long with him.

"This is Jemma," Sarah tells him. "Jemma, this is Billy." Billy comes around in front of me and smiles at me too. He has a big head, and his smile is so wide it seems to take up most of his face. But he's a friend of Dan's, so I'm sure he can't really be that nice.

"Hi, Jemma. How ya doing?" says Billy. He looks up at Sarah. "Dan's crazy about you, you know. He don't say much, but I can tell!"

Sarah laughs. "Really?"

Thanks, Billy, I think irritably. I don't need him telling her that. *Come on, Sarah. Let's go.*

"He's a good guy, you know. Takes care of his friends. Look, I gotta take off," says Billy. "Nice to see you."

Good.

"I've got to get Jemma home too," says Sarah. "She's not feeling well."

"Say hi to Dan from me," says Billy. "Hope you feel better, Jemma."

10

At last we're home, and I'm glad to be inside where it's warm. My worries slip away, and my head feels better. I enjoy a peaceful five minutes in the living room before I hear a wailing sound from outside. Mom's key is in the door, and the wailing is getting louder.

"Come on, inside," Mom is telling Olivia. I hear Finn run past and up the stairs. I think he finds Olivia's tantrums as painful as I do.

"It wasn't my fault! That boy pushed in front of me!" Olivia says, crying uncontrollably.

"You didn't have to hit him, though, did you?" Mom says.

Olivia has thrown herself on the floor and is kicking her heels and screaming at the top of her lungs, while Mom tries to calm her down. I wish I could kick and yell like that.

Mom and Olivia eventually go upstairs, and the screaming becomes more distant.

By dinnertime Olivia has calmed down. I'm still not

hungry, though. Sarah realizes this when the food she's spooning into my mouth just sits there and doesn't go down.

"Oh, Jem, you're really not well, are you? I'll take your temperature again."

I don't have a high temperature, which she soon finds out. After dinner, she leaves me in the living room with Olivia and Finn. They are changed, ready for bed, and watching TV in their robes. They look cozy and cute, curled up on either end of the sofa. It's *101 Dalmatians*, and I'm half watching too, though I'm not really interested. We've seen it dozens of times.

Someone's at the front door, and I hear Dad go to open it.

And I hear Dan's voice. He's here *again*.

"I was just passing by, and I wondered if I could have a quick word with Sarah," Dan says. "It won't take long, I promise."

I wish Dad would just tell him to buzz off. "I'll call her," Dad says.

He leaves Dan waiting in the hall and goes to look for Sarah. But of course Dan doesn't stay there. I hear his breathing as he comes into the living room. I will him to leave me alone.

"Hiya, Jemma," he says.

Olivia jumps and looks up from the TV. Finn's eyes stay firmly fixed on the screen, as if he's heard nothing.

"What are you doing here?" Olivia asks Dan.

"Just stopped by to see Sarah," Dan tells her.

"You're always stopping by," Olivia comments. "Do you love her?"

I laugh. It comes out as a snort. I'm curious to see how Dan reacts. He doesn't answer right away.

Then, "Yes, I love her," he says as though he actually means it.

Olivia giggles. "D'you wanna see me dance?" she asks.

Dan moves around and I see him nod. "Go ahead." He looks longingly at the door. Maybe he wishes he'd stayed in the hall.

Olivia turns off the TV. Finn continues staring at the blank TV screen while she puts on some ballet music. She takes off her bathrobe and begins to dance in her pink pajamas. Her steps are in perfect time, her toes pointed. Dan claps, and she is delighted with the attention.

Then Sarah comes in.

"Dan wanted to see me dance," Olivia tells her.

"She's good too," says Dan.

Olivia beams, hanging onto Dan's arm. "He loves you," she tells Sarah. "I know cuz he told me."

Sarah smiles at Dan. "What's up? It's not the best time."

He untangles himself from Olivia, pulls Sarah into his arms, and kisses her—as if that is the answer to her question.

Olivia watches, standing right next to them. She giggles loudly again. "D'you want me to kiss you like that, Finn?" She flings herself onto the sofa and pushes her lips toward him teasingly. Finn ducks and dashes upstairs.

"Can we go somewhere more private?" Dan asks. "Just for a minute. I won't keep you from your *work*."

He heads past me toward the door, and I watch anxiously as Sarah follows. She moves quickly out of sight, but I can still hear her in the hallway, telling him we bumped into Billy. They must have moved farther away or lowered their voices because I don't hear any more.

Olivia watches them go too and turns to me, her face sullen. She didn't want them to go off to talk "in private" any more than I did. She starts practicing her dance in front of me. I think she's hoping to dance for Dan again before he goes. I hope he leaves soon.

I watch Olivia dance. She looks almost angelic with her long, wavy blond hair, loose now after her bath. Usually it's tied back in a ponytail or braid.

She was in five different foster homes before she came here. *Five!* I can't begin to imagine that. She's lucky Mom and Dad have so much patience and can cope with her.

I hear Sarah and Dan in the hall. And so does Olivia. She stops midtwirl and dashes out of the room. The front door clicks before she can get there, and her screams pierce through the house as she yells at Sarah for not letting her say goodbye to Dan.

It takes Sarah at least five minutes to calm her down. "Come on, Olivia, time for bed," Sarah finally says. I can still hear the occasional muted sob.

My head is pounding from the screaming. Olivia's music is still playing, and that doesn't help either.

I sit waiting. The music finally comes to a stop. The house

is peaceful at last. I am drifting off. My headache dulls from a throb to a slight pulsing. I'm hoping that when Sarah comes to put me to bed, she'll tell me what Dan said—why he came.

Dad comes in after putting Finn to bed and puts the TV on, turning me so I am facing it.

"*Mastermind* is on," he says. "Let's see how many we can answer."

The first chosen subject is Agatha Christie. I can actually answer lots of the questions. I even get one right that the contestant gets wrong.

Mom comes in eventually and flops down on the sofa next to Dad. He puts his arm around her. Mom's cell phone rings. Dad sighs as she pulls it from her cardigan pocket.

"Hello, Paula," Mom says. "How are you, dear?" There's a long pause. "Really? Well, that's encouraging!"

"What did she say?" Dad asks after Mom puts away her phone.

"The police had a lot of calls after *Crime Watch*. Apparently they've been questioning someone today."

"Let's hope he's the one," says Dad. "It would be good to know he's off the streets."

———

Sarah is unusually quiet as she gets me ready for bed. Most likely Olivia has worn her out. Or maybe it's what Dan said to her in private when he came over. It couldn't have been Dan the police were questioning, could it? Was he telling Sarah he's a suspect? Sarah is quiet, but she doesn't seem shocked or upset. Then again, she's under Dan's spell, like everyone else, so I'm sure he could've convinced her that he had nothing to do with it. I wish she would talk to me.

11

Sarah is still quiet when she dresses me on Sunday morning. She doesn't mention Dan. Mom and Dad say nothing more about Ryan or the man the police questioned. Everyone is busy getting ready for Finn's sixth birthday.

Finn doesn't like balloons, but Dad has found some "Happy Birthday" paper decorations with alternating blue and yellow triangles. Finn is oblivious to the specialness of the day and has no interest in the birthday cards, so Olivia opens them for him. Finn is more interested in the colored envelopes and proceeds to line them up neatly across the floor. I watch him, and at one point he looks up at me and meets my eyes. Although neither of us can speak, I feel close to Finn. I always have. I sense that he likes me watching him.

Mom and Olivia bake a cake. I enjoy the bustle in the kitchen and the delicious baking smells, especially the smell of melted chocolate, which Mom lets me taste from a spoon. Olivia is happy and doing what Mom tells her for a change.

Mom is so patient with her, even when she spills sugar on the floor. While the cake's in the oven, Sarah takes Olivia for a walk to the store, and they come back with bags of little candies to decorate it with. Olivia is ecstatic. Once the cake has cooled, Mom ices it with buttercream frosting, and Olivia lines up the candies in neat rows saying, "Finn will like it like that." She puts the candles in a line across the middle.

"It looks great," she announces, and rubs her belly. "Yum, yum!"

"You'll have to wait until later," Mom warns, but once she's left the room, Olivia stays next to the cake, staring at it greedily.

She looks thoughtful, then carefully takes three candies from each row and moves the others to cover the gaps. She stuffs the ones she's taken into her mouth.

Mom comes back before Olivia can do it again. Soon it's time for Finn to open his presents.

Dad showed me his present when he bought it, and I've been looking forward to seeing Finn's reaction.

We all sit in the living room and watch as Finn opens the box with its striped wrapping paper. He pulls out a huge box of matchsticks.

They're not matches you light, but ones people use to make model ships and things like that. There's a picture of a ship on the box. When Dad showed me, I didn't get it at first. I couldn't see Finn making model ships. But then Dad took out a few matchsticks and lined them up. Dad understands Finn.

Finn examines the box, opens it, and tips all the matchsticks out. A huge grin spreads across his face. Finn rarely smiles, and I have never seen a smile as big as this. I catch Dad's eye—his grin is as big as Finn's. Finn gets busy making a line of matchsticks that stretches the length of the living room.

"Don't give me matchsticks when it's my birthday, will you?" says Olivia.

Dad laughs.

We go into the kitchen, and Mom lights the candles on the cake, but Finn is still lining up his matchsticks and won't come. In the end, Mom brings the cake carefully into the living room and Mom, Dad, Sarah, and Olivia sing "Happy Birthday." Finn doesn't even look up, but I feel suddenly happy, with the brightness of the candles and the warmth of my family around me. "You can blow the candles out for him," Mom tells Olivia, and Olivia jumps up and down with excitement.

We go back to the kitchen to eat the cake, which is delicious, and Mom keeps a piece for Finn to have later.

Two hours later, Finn and I are alone in the living room. He has moved on from lining the matchsticks up along the wall. He is now arranging them in what looks like a big square around my wheelchair—though I can only see part of it. It definitely has at least two right angles. I sense he is enclosing me completely.

Now and then he looks at me and meets my eyes as if seeking my approval. I have never seen Finn make eye contact with anyone apart from me. I like being the center of his play. I feel alive and connected in a way that is rare for me. I think Finn has completed one square, because he is now starting a second one, right around the first. He has never made anything but straight lines before. I hope Dad will come in—he's going to be so impressed. I hear footsteps, but it's Olivia who comes around in front of me, and my heart sinks.

She sometimes messes up Finn's neat lines deliberately, and I don't think she'll understand.

She gasps. "Wow, Finn! That's amazing."

She gets it! I am stunned and feel a little guilty for assuming she wouldn't. Then I hear her calling, "Everyone, come and see! Come and see what Finn's done!"

That's exactly what I wanted to do. Sometimes it happens like that—I know what I want people to do, and they do it—and it feels a little like I can control things, just for a moment. Olivia is thrilled to be the one who shares the news. Sarah appears first, then Mom and Dad.

They gather around and all "Wow!" over what Finn has done. Dad tells him it's amazing, and the others agree. I see Mom squeeze Dad's hand, and they share a smile. Finn continues, apparently oblivious, but I am sure he is pleased.

In this moment I feel full of love for them all: Mom, Dad, Sarah, Finn—and even Olivia. I don't want anything to change.

12

I was on a high after Finn's birthday until the next morning when I remembered about the college visit on Wednesday. Sarah has already started packing my bag. We're going to stay overnight—Mom, Sarah, and me in a hotel. I am looking forward to having Mom and Sarah to myself for twenty-four hours, even though I can't get rid of the worry about being sent away.

I'm trying to focus on the professor and the possibility of communication rather than the idea of actually going to Carlstone, so I feel calmer. But as the day goes on, I sense something isn't right. I've got a pain in my back and my lower stomach. I might have an infection. That's happened before, and it can get really bad if no one notices.

As Sarah wheels me into the kitchen at dinnertime I hear Mom telling Dad that the police have charged the man they were questioning.

"That's good news," says Sarah. "Who was it? Do they know why he did it?"

"Why who did what?" Olivia demands, coming in. Mom gives Sarah a look as if she shouldn't be asking such things in front of Olivia, which is a little unfair since Olivia just sneaked in and it was Mom who brought it up. I want to know more details too, but Dad changes the subject and starts marveling about Finn's amazing matchstick squares again. It's so frustrating.

Olivia glowers. Everyone tenses. She's like a lit firework that'll go off with a bang at any moment.

Dad tries to distract her by asking her what she'd like for her birthday. She turns to him, her eyes wide with excitement. It's not her birthday for three months, but this doesn't seem to matter as she takes a deep breath and starts to reel off a very long list. A TV for her room, an iPad, a bigger dollhouse. Then Olivia adds, "That's if I'm still here."

Mom and Dad look at her in astonishment. "Of course you'll still be here, love," says Dad. "This is your home. You're not going anywhere."

"I'm not sure I can promise you any of those things for your birthday, though," Mom adds quickly, catching Dad's eye. "You'll have to wait and see."

I suddenly realize that Olivia can rarely have had more than one birthday in the same place. It must be hard for her to trust that she's really here to stay.

At least Dad has successfully distracted her from Sarah's question about the murder suspect. I'm still thinking about it, though. Who have the police charged? If it's Dan, Sarah will hear about it soon. Or is it someone else altogether?

During the night I kept thinking about it until the pain in my stomach got so bad that I was only thinking about that. Now it's there all the time rather than coming and going. I was willing Sarah to notice this morning, because I can usually rely on her to pick up on it when something's not right. But she seemed distracted.

At school, I am uncomfortable all day. Then something happens that stops me from thinking about the pain altogether. About an hour after we get home, Mom asks where Finn is. No one can find him.

Mom is looking upstairs, Dad is downstairs, and Sarah is in the backyard. Olivia is "helping" but clearly getting bored. Dad's searched every closet twice, including the one under the stairs.

Mom comes down. Her hair is all over the place, and her eyes are panicky. "He's not here," she mutters. "He must have gone outside. He's not here!"

Dad soothes her, stroking her back. "He's around here somewhere. I'm sure of it. You know how good he is at hiding. He can't open the front door."

"Maybe he slipped out when someone opened it," says Mom. She puts her hand to her mouth. "I went out the back door to put out some trash. Could he have gotten out then?"

"He's not in the backyard," says Dad, "and you didn't

unlock the gate, did you? He's not tall enough to climb over it without standing on something."

"Finn?" Mom calls. She's trying to sound calm, but there's a rough edge to her voice. "Come on out, dear! You're definitely the hide-and-seek winner."

Mom and Dad are quiet, waiting, listening. There's a sound on the stairs. Mom dashes around the banister.

"Oh, Olivia! No sign of Finn?"

"He's probably gone out and walked into the street," Olivia announces. "He has no idea how to cross streets, does he?"

I hear Mom let out a gasp.

"That's enough, Olivia," says Dad.

"I've been looking for him," Olivia protests. "Looking and looking. Just as hard as everyone else—except Jemma." She's come into view now and gives a glance in my direction.

I am sitting in the living room, facing out toward the hallway. I have been sitting like this the whole time, facing the closet under the stairs—the closet where Finn has been hiding for over an hour. I know he's there. I saw him go in. He must be curled up so far into the dark back corner that Dad's two expeditions inside have failed to discover him.

Dad goes out to walk the streets, though I'm sure he still thinks that Finn is in the house.

"He'll turn up," Sarah assures Mom.

"You're *sure* nothing happened—nothing that upset him?" Mom asks Sarah.

I look at Sarah's face. Although she helps out with Finn and Olivia, her job is caring for me. Mom's not being fair.

"I told you," Sarah says sharply, "he seemed fine to me. He was lining up cars in his room." Sarah looks like she's going to cry. I want to tell her Mom's just worried and doesn't really blame her.

When Dad comes back, Mom wants to call the police. Dad wants to wait. They argue. Mom starts really shouting. It's awful. If only I could tell them. If only Finn would come out. I try to make a noise—gurgling noises that turn into *Ugghh, ugghh*.

Dad then blames Mom for upsetting me. I've just made things worse.

Sarah comes to comfort me. "Don't worry, Finn will be fine," she assures me.

In the end, Dad phones the police.

I know that Finn must be able to hear this. He knows who the police are, though I'm not sure if he understands enough to realize the worry he's causing.

I wonder why he's hiding. He only does it when he's really stressed out. Once he hid when his teacher was off sick and he didn't like the substitute teacher. Perhaps the packing has upset him, and he's worried about us being away. That must be it.

Last time, he was found after twenty minutes. He was at the back of Mom and Dad's closet, behind the shoe rack.

Dad says the police are on their way. Mom calls Social Services too. They have to know he is missing. I feel so sorry for Mom. I'm sure she's worried they'll think she's not taking care of us.

The doorbell rings.

"That was quick," says Mom, rushing to answer.

I hear a voice I don't recognize and strain to hear the words. It's not the police; it's the window cleaner wanting to be paid.

"Sorry," Mom says, sounding frazzled. "Do you mind coming back? We're having a bit of a crisis. You haven't seen a small boy wandering down the street, have you?"

I don't hear the answer. "Oh, look, it's not fair to you. I'll grab my purse," Mom says. She comes into the living room and picks up her bag without even glancing at me.

"That's funny, I'm sure I had more than that," she says to herself. "Ben! Do you have a ten handy?"

"Sure," calls Dad. "Really, couldn't he have waited?"

As Dad goes to the door, Mom looks like she's holding back tears.

When Dad comes back, he persuades her to sit down and have a cup of tea while we wait for the police. He pushes me into the kitchen and Mom sits, head in hands, at the table, while Dad puts the kettle on.

Sarah comes in too, followed by a sulky-looking Olivia.

"Let me do that," Sarah tells Dad, getting some mugs out of the cupboard.

"Can I have a cookie?" Olivia asks, spying the package on the shelf above the mugs.

"Please," Dad reminds her.

Dad pulls down the package and opens it. He stares for a moment at the cookies.

"Can I have one, *pleeeeaaaase*?" Olivia demands.

"I think I'll get out the chocolate chip cookies," Dad says loudly.

That's a little weird. I think the stress has gotten to him. Olivia gives him a confused look. And then it clicks. He's trying to tempt Finn out. Chocolate chips are Finn's favorite. He always has to have three so that he can line them up.

Dad puts three on Olivia's plate, and she beams. "I'll put three on a plate here for Finn," Dad says.

"Oh... The cookies are for *Finn*."

Finn walks into the kitchen and sits down, grabbing all three cookies tightly. He doesn't meet anyone's eyes, but that's not unusual.

"Where have you been?" Mom demands as gently as she can manage.

She knows he won't answer, but I see her shoulders relax with relief as she turns to Dad with a smile.

13

The crisis has passed, and the house has gone from panic to calm. Soon it is as if nothing happened. Everyone's back doing their own thing, and I am back with the pain that has somehow spread while I wasn't thinking about it and is definitely getting worse.

I wish I could focus on something else to put it out of my mind. I try to concentrate on the TV, and then Sarah comes in with a basket of clothes to fold and I watch her as she bends and folds at the edge of my vision. My thoughts go back to Dan and the murder. Sarah looks busy but relaxed. It can't be Dan who's been charged. She would have heard something by now, wouldn't she? But just because they've charged someone, that doesn't mean they've definitely got the right man, does it?

A program comes on about people who are training for the next Paralympics. There's a woman with cerebral palsy who is hoping to compete in archery, and even though I'll never do anything like that, it is inspiring to watch her. She's spent hours and hours each week practicing to get this good, and she looks so determined.

Still, it's difficult to concentrate. The pain won't go away. I try thinking about Jodi instead—about her letter and how amazing it would be to get another one. But nothing's come. I hope she hasn't changed her mind.

I'd love so much to be able to communicate with her. The professor guy who's coming to Carlstone—could he have the answer for me? Even though the college thing is scary, the idea that I might be able to communicate is so huge that most of the time I don't let myself think about it. All through my life, people have tried different things—from pointing at letter boards to eye-gaze technology—but nothing has worked. I remember when I was ten, and we all got excited because a new teacher taught me to say yes and no by blinking. But then I got really sick with an infection. I was in hospital for a long time, and when I felt better, I couldn't control my blinking anymore.

Is there really a chance? I have so much I want to say—but I'm scared to hope. What if by the time I met my sister I could actually do it? When Sarah goes on about Dan, I could interrupt her and tell her exactly what he's really like. When Finn hides, I could tell them where he is or tempt him out myself with cookies. And right now I could say that I'm in pain and where it hurts.

I know even if there is a way, it won't be easy. I found it hard enough with the blinking. It took a lot of effort to control it. And all the questions made me feel panicky. I was used to watching, not deciding, and if I didn't respond quickly, people either kept repeating the question over and over, which was infuriating, or just gave up, which was even worse. And of course nobody ever asked me the questions I wanted them to ask.

Sometimes I blinked by accident and gave an answer I didn't intend. I blinked "no" when Mom asked if I'd like ketchup, and ever since, for the last four years, she's stopped giving it to me. I don't like it on everything, but I really do like it on fries.

At least when I could blink I was able to show how much I knew and understood. They were amazed to see that I could read. I had a teacher at school when I was six, Miss Moray, who taught us all as if we were as bright as any other six-year-olds. She went through all the letters and basic words. My next teacher didn't bother with reading at all, but I've always read signs and labels, and Mom often put the subtitles on the TV too. What I found hard was making choices. Mom said she'd always known how bright I was, but I think she was the only one. Even Dad had never seemed sure, although he'd tried hard not to show it.

It's hard to admit, but after I couldn't control the blinking, part of me felt relieved. It was a relief to go back to just watching and not having to decide. But it's different now. I'd give anything for the chance to be able to do it again. I'm older, and there's so much I want to say. I want to talk to Jodi. I want to make my own choices. *Yes* and *no* won't be enough, though, not to tell them about Dan.

This woman I'm watching has been training hard, and she's studying in college too. Her disability is much milder than mine, but it is still impressive to watch. And she's putting in all that effort with no certainty that she'll even make it onto the Paralympic team. It's all about daring to hope, isn't it? You have to dare to think you might win. If I dare to think I might communicate again, it might come true.

But it might not. And the disappointment would be a million times harder.

The pain in my back is getting worse—a constant dull throb.

Sarah's phone rings. It's Richard. Sarah is still upset, thinking Mom blames her for Finn going missing. She's telling Richard about it. "No, no," she says—and I think he might have suggested coming over. "I don't have any time off until the weekend," she tells him. "I'll be fine. It helps to talk to you. You've made me feel much better."

She's no sooner put down her phone than it rings again. She answers without even looking at the screen.

"R–Dan, hi!" She doesn't tell him about Finn. "What, now?" she says. "I can't. I've got to put Jemma to bed soon. And to be honest, I'm worn out. I've had such a crap day..."

I wonder what he's saying. "No, no, you can't," Sarah tells him.

Dan's not like Richard, though. He won't take no for an answer.

Sarah puts her phone down and sighs. "He's coming over," she tells me. "It's not that I don't want to see him; it's just that I'm so tired."

So now I know for sure—the police haven't arrested Dan. It must be someone else.

Mom comes downstairs, and Sarah explains to her that Dan is stopping by. From the abrupt tone of her voice, Mom is clearly not happy.

"He won't be here long, I promise," says Sarah. "I tried to tell him not to come, but he insisted."

"What a day," Mom says, sighing. "I feel like I'm going mad. Oh, Sarah—you didn't borrow money from my purse, did you?"

"What? No, I didn't. Why would I have done that?" Sarah demands.

"I know you buy things for Jemma sometimes, and I thought you might—"

"I wouldn't without asking!" Sarah retorts.

"Forget I said anything," Mom says sheepishly. "I probably spent it without realizing."

Sarah is silent. I feel so powerless. The tension between them hurts me inside and frightens me, but there's nothing I can do. If Sarah's not happy here, if she stops getting along with Mom, then she won't want to stay.

Dan arrives half an hour later. I am still up and in the living room. Mom and Dad are upstairs. I have a partial view into the hall, and I am shocked to see Dan grab Sarah as she opens the door. For a moment I think he's going to hurt her, but he pulls her toward him and kisses her hard. Sarah moves back, laughing awkwardly.

"What's up, babe?" he asks, flinching as if reeling from her rejection.

"Nothing's up," Sarah tells him. She's speaking quietly— but not too quietly for me to hear. "I've told you... You can't keep turning up like this. You know what Lorraine—"

"And I've told you, I can't keep away, babe!" says Dan. "Have you thought about what I said?"

"You know how I feel about you," Sarah says softly. "But I have to be here overnight for Jemma. I can't live at your place."

"Give up the job! I'll take care of you." It's Dan who's speaking quietly now.

My heart lurches. She won't do that, will she?

I listen hard to hear her reply. She starts with a kiss, which doesn't feel like a good sign. I wish Mom hadn't given her such a hard time. She's feeling fed up here, and now Dan's offering her a way out. But what about me?

"I want to be with you, but Jemma needs me," Sarah tells him, and I heave a sigh of relief that comes out as a slight snort. Dan turns toward the living-room doorway and meets my eyes briefly with a look of disgust.

"They'll get someone else, no problem," he says, turning back to Sarah. "There are lots of people wanting aide jobs."

"I like my job," Sarah argues.

"Do you, though? Really?" Dan is shaking his head. "You've got the patience of a saint, babe, but no one does this kind of job unless they have to."

I feel my muscles tighten.

Sarah pauses. "I... Look, let's talk about it more the next time I see you."

"I'll take you out. When're you free?" Dan demands.

"Hang on, I'll check," Sarah tells him.

She's gone to check her days on the calendar, and my worst fear comes true. Dan comes into the living room. He stands close—bends over me—staring at me, screwing up his nose. Then he shakes his head.

"You think she's gonna stay here, don't you? But you just wait—"

At that moment, his cell phone rings and he moves away as he answers it. I can breathe again, though I'm horrified by the way he spoke to me.

"Hiya, Billy! What's up, man?" he says. His voice is quiet but brash, different from the cheerful, friendly one he uses with Sarah, and not that nasty voice he uses for me.

"Yeah! It's all worked out? Behind the grocery store? I know where you mean... Sure thing. See ya."

He puts the phone in his pocket just as Sarah comes back.

"I've got next Thursday off," she tells him.

"That's over a week away! You can stay over, though, right?"

She nods and gives him a nudge toward the door, telling him he has to go now. He jokes that she's always trying to get rid of him, and Sarah rolls her eyes and points upstairs, as though it's because of Mom. Dan whispers something in Sarah's ear and gives her another kiss.

I'm so relieved when he's gone.

"He loves me, Jemma," Sarah says dreamily a little later as she carefully brushes my teeth. She's supporting my head with her other hand in case I suddenly jolt. "And I love him too."

I feel sick. I wish I could tell her he's a disgusting creep. "Big day tomorrow," she says, changing the subject. "Bet you're excited!"

I'd almost forgotten about the college visit. I wonder what the professor will say. Is there really a chance...?

14

"*Have you seen Jemma's red* fleece?" Sarah calls to Mom. It's chaos this morning as Sarah runs around finding last-minute things to put in my suitcase. I seem to need an awful lot of stuff for an overnight stay.

Mom is trying to finish her own packing, and Dad is attempting to single-handedly get Olivia and Finn ready for school. My back and stomach pain are even worse, and I have this kind of fuzzy, giddy feeling. It's definitely an infection. Sarah thinks it's just anxiety about the day ahead. Typical. When I was anxious before, they thought it was physical, and now it's the other way around.

"Here it is," says Mom, handing my fleece to Sarah.

Mom turns to me and looks concerned. "There's no need for you to be worried about today—I promise." The pain in my back has developed into a throb, and it is spreading outward, surging through me.

I feel hot—too hot.

Someone's speaking. Sarah is moving closer.

I think she says, "Something's not right," but the words sound blurry. Her face, close to mine, is blurry too. Everything is spinning.

I am vaguely aware of being lifted out of my wheelchair, faces bending over me, voices talking. Then the jolting movement of the ambulance, the gurney, the white curtains swishing, bright lights, the IV, the monitor. These are all familiar to me. I've spent a lot of time at this hospital.

Mom is sitting by my bed now, holding my hand. Her hand is warm and safe. I drift off and wake to find the hand holding mine is larger, firmer. Mom has been replaced by Dad. Later it is a smaller, long-fingered hand, as Sarah chats away to me.

Mom jokes about the convenience of living only a ten-minute drive from the hospital. It wasn't something she or Dad thought about when they bought the house years ago, but it has proven very useful.

Mom, Dad, and Sarah set up a rotation. There is always someone by my side. I am so glad they are there. I would completely panic otherwise. Some nurses do stuff without even bothering to talk to me, as if there's no point explaining anything. Whoever's with me will ask and make sure I know what's going to happen. I'd be terrified if some stranger just lifted my arm and started putting a needle in me or something.

Sarah squeezes my hand. She seems agitated. I can feel her pulse faster than it should be.

"You awake, Jem?" she says, seeing my eyes open. "How're you feeling? The pain should be better after all the stuff they're pumping into you."

She gives a nod toward the drip and smiles.

She's right. The pain is better, though I feel very weak and my head feels heavy and peculiar.

"I'm so sorry I didn't realize how bad it was, Jemma," she tells me, giving my hand another squeeze. "Your mom blames me for not spotting it earlier. I feel awful."

Sarah thinks Mom blamed her for Finn going missing and now for this. I wish Mom would stop accusing her.

It's only the next day, when my head is a little clearer, that I realize I missed the trip to the college. I'm not going to meet the professor.

Mom seems to realize what I'm thinking.

"Don't worry, dear. We'll rearrange the trip. I actually spoke to Professor Spalding, and he said he'd be very interested in meeting you."

She isn't saying, "And he's sure he can help." But at least there is still a chance.

I'm dozing, aware that Sarah is holding my hand. She's been here for a long time. When I manage to open my eyes briefly, I see that hers are half-closing. Then suddenly there's a voice. Someone else is in the room.

"Hi, babe," he says. My stomach clenches.

Sarah sits up and turns around.

"What are you doing here?" she asks. It's something she seems to say to Dan a lot.

"I was worried about you—sitting here for hours on end. And I was right to worry, wasn't I? Look at you. You're exhausted."

"I'm okay," Sarah says.

"Yeah, sure," he says, raising his eyebrows in disbelief. "Come on, let me take you for a coffee."

"But I can't leave Jemma," Sarah says, sounding shocked that he would suggest it.

"She'll be all right," says Dan. "It's not like she can run off or anything."

"Dan!" Sarah exclaims.

"Tell you what. I'll stay with Jemma while you get a coffee," says Dan. "That way she won't be on her own, and you get a break. Win, win."

"I shouldn't...but... Oh, babe, would you really do that?" Sarah asks. He leans forward and kisses her. If there was ever a time when I most wanted Sarah's mind-reading skills to kick in, this would be it. With every thought, I urge her to stay. I want her to see it in my eyes. But she's not even looking at me.

"If you're worried at all, press that button to reach the nurses' station," Sarah tells him. "I'm sure she'll be fine, though."

She turns to me, stroking my arm. I stare at her, hoping she will see the distress on my face. I even try to make a sound, but just a horrid *erhhhhh* comes out.

"I'll be back in five minutes, I promise," she assures me.

Then she's gone.

15

Dan doesn't sit down beside my bed and hold my hand—which is a relief. Instead, he paces around the bed slowly. I begin to wish he would sit down. I am happier when I can see him than when I can't, and when he's on the other side of the bed, I can't see him at all. Now he's back on this side.

Is he really here because he can't bear to be apart from Sarah, or is he checking up on her?

He fixes me with a sarcastic smile. "Always causing trouble, aren't you, Jemma? It would be much easier if they just kept you here. Or..."

He's moved back from the bed, and he seems to be looking closely at everything—the tube going into me from the drip with antibiotics, the plugs in the wall.

I can see what he's doing. He's trying to upset me again, pretending to look for a way to switch me off! At least, I hope he's pretending.

No! He's crouching by the wall. *He's actually doing it! I*

want Sarah. I need Sarah. A gurgling noise comes from deep in my throat. Dan stands up, holding a plug in his hand, laughing. "What's that? Is that the best you can do for a scream?"

Then I realize the lamp beside my bed has gone off. He's pulled out the plug! I shouldn't have panicked. Of course, I'm not on a life-support machine. I was just so scared of him... I know he wants me out of the way. He wants Sarah to himself.

He pushes the plug back in and chuckles as the light flickers on.

I wish Sarah would come back. It must have been five minutes by now.

He comes nearer, sits down on the chair by my bed. I listen to his heavy breathing. I wait, unsure what he's going to do next. He's still looking around. I can see his eyes on the box of disposable gloves. Now he's looking behind me. Does he have his eye on my pillow? Am I imagining it, or is he still thinking of ways...?

"All okay?"

Sarah's voice is such a welcome relief that I feel myself sink back against the softness of the bed. The thudding in my chest slows down.

"Yeah, Jemma's been just fine," Dan assures her.

"It was so sweet of you to do this," Sarah says, kissing him.

"Anytime," Dan tells her, "no prob." He kisses her back. Dan leaves, giving me a parting smile that makes my heart shudder. Sarah sits down, and soon a nurse comes in to check my pulse, temperature, and blood pressure.

She tuts. "Pulse is higher than it should be," she comments. "I'll get a doctor to check her."

"Dan got your pulse up?" Sarah teases. "You don't have a thing for him, do you? He's all mine, Jemma!"

If only I could tell her...

Mom arrives at that moment and is concerned to hear about my pulse, fussing over me.

"Did you notice anything?" Mom asks Sarah. "Has she been awake or asleep?"

Sarah scowls. Mom is being pretty aggressive with the questions. Luckily, Sarah is saved from answering by the doctor. He takes my pulse again, and it's already going back to normal. My temperature and blood pressure are fine.

"Nothing to worry about," he says, smiling at Mom and then at me.

Sarah leaves without saying goodbye to Mom.

There's a strange feeling when I am finally back home. It's hard to explain, but it's as if things have shifted while I've been away, even though it was only a couple of days. One of the chairs in the living room has been moved around, and there's a small spiky plant in a pot on the hall shelf. It wasn't there before. There's always been a china elephant on that shelf and nothing else, but he's been pushed to the side and the spiky plant is in the middle. Am I getting as bad as Finn—not liking any change?

The second, far more important thing is that Sarah isn't here. Mom gave her extra time off because she'd spent so much time at the hospital with me. Sarah's gone to stay with Dan, like he wanted.

I want her here, and I'm worried about her being alone with him. She has no idea what he's really like. What if she lets something slip about going to the concert with Richard? What if Dan already knows that something is going on?

Finn comes in, and I hope for some sign that he's pleased I'm back. Maybe I should know better, but I've always felt we understand each other. I can hear him moving about behind me, but he doesn't let me see him. Then I hear a sound I've heard before.

Bang, bang, bang.

He is banging his head against the wall—rhythmically, over and over.

"Stop, Finn!" I want to yell. Finn used to do this a lot. But for the last two years he's done it much less. I think me being away and the change to his routine may have really upset him. Perhaps that's why he's staying there behind me. He wants me to know he's angry. I feel so bad. I don't want to upset Finn.

"Oh, Finn! There's no need for that," says Mom, coming into the living room. "Let's find something for you to play with."

My muscles relax as Mom takes the matchsticks out of the cupboard and Finn starts lining them up.

"Look what's come today!" Mom is waving an envelope at me.

I get a gush of happiness as I watch her open it.

A letter! A letter from Jodi. Mom begins reading:

Dear Jemma,

I was so excited when your mom wrote and said she had read my letter to you. I hope you were as happy as I was to find out you have a sister!

She says she really hopes to find a way for you to communicate so you can write back or even talk to me one day. That would be so cool. I looked online, and I found stuff about head pointers and eye-gaze technology—it all sounds so clever! I've been reading up about cerebral palsy too. I really want to understand what it's like.

I've printed out a photo of Fluff this time. I hope your mom will send me one of you.

I hope we will be able to meet one day soon!

Love, Jodi

"She sounds great, doesn't she, Jemma?" Mom says, sighing. "I know she's eager to meet you, and I'm sure you'd like to meet her too, but I still think it's best to take things slowly. I'd like to see Professor Spalding first."

Finn has stopped lining up sticks and is sitting, rocking.

I understand what Mom's saying. It would be amazing to be able to "talk" to Jodi somehow. Even just with a *yes* and a *no*. But I don't know how long I'd have to wait. I want to meet Jodi now.

16

When Dan drops Sarah off the next day, Mom thanks him for the plant he bought. No wonder I didn't like it.

"You're looking so much better, Jem," Sarah tells me, smiling warmly. We're in the bathroom, and Sarah has just emptied my bag. "You gave me a scare, you really did."

I gave myself a scare too. But right now I'm more interested in whether Sarah had her talk with Dan about moving in.

"Your mom was telling me that the professor guy is going to be back at Carlstone College next Thursday," Sarah continues, "just for a day. After that he's abroad for three months. I think we should go for it, if you're feeling well enough."

I'm still feeling tired after my infection, but I do want to meet him. Even if there's only a small chance of anything changing. Now that Mom's fixed on me meeting him before she'll let me meet Jodi, I have an even greater incentive than before. But if he can't help me, will I still get to meet her?

Sarah is pushing me toward the kitchen for dinner when she stops and I jolt in the chair. Her phone is ringing upstairs.

"I'll just get it... It might be Dan. I won't be a sec." She leaves me outside the kitchen. Mom's not in there, but I can see Olivia through the doorway. She's on a stool by the kitchen counter. What is she up to? She climbs onto the countertop and opens a high cupboard, the one where Mom keeps the candy. She has a bag of gummy bears in her hand as she jumps down, and I see her stash them in the pocket of her jeans.

Sarah is back. "It was Richard," she whispers, "about the concert. I can't wait!"

I'm glad she's confiding in me again. It feels more normal. For a moment I imagine that I'm going with Sarah instead of Richard. I'd definitely be just as excited as she is. I've seen concerts on TV, and I think it would be amazing to hear a band live, especially Glowlight.

It is mac and cheese for dinner. I like pasta, but cheese sauce sometimes gets stuck in my throat and makes me cough. Sarah is feeding me. Finn's not eating but is rocking backward and forward in his chair. He's not so enthusiastic about pasta either—maybe because it is so curvy—especially macaroni. Olivia has wolfed hers down.

She looks at Sarah. "Do you like staying all night with Dan?" She giggles.

"Yeah, I had a great time, thanks," Sarah tells her.

"Did you have sex?" Olivia asks.

I cough up some cheese sauce.

"Olivia!" Dad splutters. "You don't ask people questions like that."

"I was just interested." Olivia's mouth turns sulky. I stop coughing. Sarah wipes my mouth with a kitchen towel and gives me a drink. Her cheeks are pink.

"How was school?" Dad asks Olivia.

"Melissa's not my friend anymore," Olivia tells him.

"I didn't know you had a friend named Melissa," Mom comments.

"She was only my friend for one day, and now she's not," says Olivia.

"Why's that?" asks Dad.

"I don't wanna talk about it." Olivia folds her arms.

Dad turns his attention to trying to coax Finn to eat. He has a few mouthfuls.

"I think we should take Jemma to meet that guy," Sarah tells Mom. "She seems to have made a good recovery, haven't you, Jemma?"

"That's great," says Mom, and she actually gives Sarah what looks like a genuine smile. "I think so too."

I'm relieved that the decision is made—and even more relieved to see Mom and Sarah talking normally to each other. Olivia and Finn go off to play while Sarah finishes feeding me and Dad turns on the radio for the news.

I'm not really listening until I catch the name Ryan Blake. Dad turns it up and shushes everyone.

"Jay Wiggins, who was charged last week with the murder of Ryan Blake, has been released after a witness came forward corroborating his alibi. The twenty-five-year-old auto mechanic had been in custody for a week. He described his relief that his name has been cleared, saying that the whole experience had been a 'complete nightmare.'"

Sarah's phone, now in her pocket, rings even before the news item has finished.

"Sorry," she says, taking it out and looking as if she is switching it off.

"Jay Wiggins?" says Dad. "Is he someone Paula knew about? Did she ever mention him?"

"Not that I can recall," says Mom.

"Well, looks like the police got it wrong. Hopefully he's not the only suspect they identified."

Maybe they do have another suspect. Maybe it's Dan. Sarah says nothing about it, of course, as she gets me ready for bed. She starts reading me a vampire romance book. I like it, and it makes for a change from Agatha Christie.

Her phone keeps buzzing as she reads. I get a glimpse of the screen one time it does as she picks it up. I see Dan's name. It's there, and then it fades away again.

17

I doze on and off for most of the drive to Carlstone College. Mom has decided we will do it in a day, so we leave really early. Anytime I open my eyes, Sarah is either texting or looking at her phone. When I wake up again, I'm refreshed, if a little stiff. We've arrived.

Mom lowers the ramp, and Sarah detaches the wheelchair from its clamps and wheels me down.

"Thank God the traffic was good," Mom comments.

"And the sun's come out for us too," adds Sarah.

I share their optimism as I am turned to face the college building. It is modern and bigger than I expected. I'd had an image in my mind from a movie set in an old boarding school. This is nothing like that.

The glass doors open automatically as we approach, and we are welcomed by the smiling woman at the reception desk. She tells us to take a seat and wait.

Sarah wheels me into a space beside some seats, and she and Mom sit down.

Opposite me I can see a sign on the wall that says CARLSTONE COLLEGE: CENTER OF EXCELLENCE FOR AUGMENTATIVE AND ALTERNATIVE COMMUNICATION. I've heard Mom talking about AAC, and I know it has to do with communication systems for people who can't speak, but I never knew what it stood for until now. I don't know what *augmentative* means, though.

Students pass us—some in wheelchairs and others walking. They all look much older than me. I wonder what it would be like to be a student here. I have to admit I get a tingle of excitement at the thought before the fear and worries about everything it would mean take over. I won't think about all that now. Instead, I distract myself by wondering what the professor will look like. I don't have to wait long to find out.

A tall man with thick, curly hair comes striding toward us.

"You must be Jemma," he says, crouching to make eye contact. "I'm very pleased to meet you." He attempts to shake my stiff, curled hand. He has kind eyes, and he is looking deeply into mine. I feel slightly afraid. My eyes give nothing away—I know that.

He turns to greet Mom and Sarah. I'm glad he spoke to me first.

"Follow me," he tells us.

We follow him down a wide corridor. There are ramps

everywhere, and the ride is smooth. The big windows throw squares of brightness onto the clean red floor.

We stop at a door, which Professor Spalding opens and holds for us as we all go in.

The room is like a doctor's office, with a desk, a computer, and chairs. There is a spiky plant on the windowsill. I hope that isn't a bad omen.

"I very much hope I can help you, Jemma," he tells me. "As you know, new communication systems are being developed all the time."

"Yes," says Mom. "We've tried various kinds of AAC with Jemma and also with our son who has severe autism. To be honest, we haven't had much luck with either of them."

Professor Spalding nods. "But you believe Jemma understands cause and effect?"

"Definitely," says Mom. "She was able to communicate 'yes' and 'no' by blinking when she was ten. She was taught to read, and we know that she understands a huge amount. We're sure she laughs sometimes too." Mom goes on to explain more of my history. Then she adds, "I know some of these communication systems can be expensive, but Jemma does have some funds from a medical negligence case. The money pays for her to have her own aide. It's not a bottomless pit, though."

"Hmmm," says Professor Spalding, tapping his pencil on the table. "We can worry about funding later. I'd like to do a few tests that will help me assess the best means of communication for you, Jemma. You must understand that even if we find a way, it will take some time to master. Babies learn to speak by making sounds, babbling, and then gradually learning to express words. Even though your understanding may be good, it will not be easy for you to put phrases together, select words, and so on. You will have to be patient."

Patience is something I know plenty about—though I am feeling impatient now. I wish he'd stop talking and get on with it.

He tries to get me to look left and right. The first time he asks, I am able to do it. He looks so pleased.

But when he asks me to repeat it, I can't. I try. I try so hard. I see the pleasure turn to disappointment as the light in his eyes fades.

He tries to see if I can move anything else—tilt my head, lift a finger, clench a cheek, open and close my mouth. My body sometimes moves. My head jolts. I automatically close my mouth to swallow food, but I cannot do it voluntarily. He asks me to make sounds too, but I can't—not intentionally.

He even tells a bad joke about a chicken, but it isn't funny enough to make me laugh. I can only laugh spontaneously; I can't make it happen.

He soon realizes what I already know. I have no control.

18

"What makes you so certain that Jemma's brain is unaffected by her illness?" the professor asks Mom and Sarah.

I can't see their faces, but I know they both believe in me.

"It's an instinct," says Mom. "We both feel it."

"Yes," Sarah agrees.

"My husband too," says Mom. "And the doctors said at the time there was no reason why her brain should have been affected."

Professor Spalding touches his lip and looks at me thoughtfully.

What is he thinking? Does he think I'm brain-dead?

"Can you sniff for me, Jemma?" he asks.

Sniff? I think he's crazy now.

"Breathe in through your nose—as hard as you can," he tells me.

For a moment I panic, and I can't think how. It's not something I've ever thought about. It's also so rare that anyone actually asks me to *do* anything. Then I calm myself. I have to hurry, or he might give up.

I sniff.

"Now breathe out through your nose."

I can do that too—though I'd love to know where he's going with this.

"Now again," he says.

I breathe in and out through my nose. I am pleased to be able to actually respond, but also confused. Everybody knows that I can breathe.

"Hmmm," says Professor Spalding. "Interesting." He pauses.

"I don't think the eye movements are going to be useful," he tells me, turning to Mom and Sarah too. "They are not consistent enough. However, a colleague of mine is developing a new communication tool based on sniffing. It's hard to tell if Jemma would have enough control, but it might be worth a try."

"Communicate with sniffing?" Sarah repeats. "I've never heard of that!"

I sniff again, just to make sure they know I can do it. Professor Spalding continues. "My colleague Alon Katz and his team are based in Israel. When he's here next, perhaps he could meet you and see if it might be suitable. We hope he'll be here in a few months."

A few months! That's so long!

Could I really use sniffing to communicate, though? Would I be able to say the things I want and need to say? I think about Dan. Can you sniff that someone is a murderer?

19

After lunch, Catherine, the assistant dean of the college, shows us around. She has beautiful shiny dark hair and a warm smile, and she is so bubbly and jokey with the students that I sense she loves working here.

"We have students using all kinds of AAC devices," she tells us. She introduces us to some of the students. One girl, who is only able to raise one eyebrow, proudly shows us that she can select words on a computer and move between screens for different categories of words. She raises her eyebrow repeatedly until the pointer reaches the word she wants on the screen, and then she stops. After a second, the word appears on the line below. Then she continues. It's very slow, but eventually she types, I GO MUSIC, and a voice speaks her words.

"Don't let us hold you up, Kaya!" says Catherine.

Then she adds, "Kaya's a total music geek."

I feel a gut-wrenching pull. How amazing it would be to spell out words on a screen like that! Would I be able to do it—by sniffing? Is it possible? We see the bedrooms and bathrooms, which are bright and spacious. Two students share each room, so I realize I'd have a roommate if I came here.

Mom says, "I think this would be a fantastic place for you in a few years. What do you think, Jemma?"

Sarah smiles at me too.

Catherine and Mom start discussing funding applications, but I am thinking about what she said. *A few years!* They weren't planning to send me here sooner. I was worrying for no reason.

On the drive home, I start to feel giddy. Sarah notices I am flushed and gets Mom to pull over. My temperature is up. She gives me medicine. We have to stop three times. I feel every jolt and jerk of the car. Then we are stuck in traffic.

"She doesn't look well," Mom moans. "This was a mistake."

"We didn't know the traffic would be like this," says Sarah. "It's just bad luck."

"I wasn't sure," says Mom. "I thought it might be too soon, but you convinced me."

"You said you felt the same!" Sarah protests, her voice getting louder and higher. "We both wanted to do it. Stop blaming me for stuff!"

"Calm down," says Mom, even though her voice is just as agitated. "I wasn't... Look, we both want the best for Jemma. Let's not fight about it."

Sarah is silent. My skin feels prickly. I feel like crying when they argue.

At last the traffic clears and we are moving, though the horrible atmosphere in the car isn't going anywhere. But I feel worse—hot and sick. My clothes are sticking to me.

When we finally get home, we are greeted by Dad. He looks washed out. He frowns with concern when he sees how flushed I am. He's so pale. And I'm only adding to his worries.

Sarah puts me to bed although the clock on the wall says it's only 6:00 p.m.

"I'm sure you'll feel better after a good rest, Jem," she tells me. "I'll keep a close eye on you. We don't want another stint in that hospital, do we?"

No, we certainly don't. The image of Dan holding up the plug he'd pulled out flashes through my head.

"I'm sorry if today was too much," Sarah says, gently bathing my hot forehead with a cool cloth. "I'm sure you'll be fine after a good night's sleep. The college was great, wasn't it?"

It is a relief to be surrounded by the softness of my bed after the jolting of the wheelchair in the car. I feel better already. My eyes close, but I don't want to sleep. I want Sarah to stay with me. I feel safe with her here, and, while she's with me, I also know she's safe from Dan. It's not much, but it's the only way I can protect her. But my eyes are closing, and I hear her footsteps on the stairs.

She left my door open, and pieces of conversation drift my way from the kitchen. Mom is telling Dad about the day. It takes a while. Then Mom says, "Everything all right here?"

"Not really," I hear Dad say. I strain to listen.

"I dropped them at school and went to work," he tells Mom, "and then I got a call to say Olivia had attacked a boy and I'd have to come and get her. She must have hit him hard... He's lost a tooth."

"*What?*" Mom exclaims. "Have you talked to her about it? Did she tell you what happened?"

"She said it wasn't her fault. I asked if he hit her first, and she said, 'No, you just don't get it,' and she wouldn't talk to me after that. She's been sulking in her room most of the day. They've suspended her until Monday."

I hear breathing close by, and my eyes open. I assume it's Sarah, back to check on me, but it's Olivia I see standing in my doorway. The light in the hall behind her means she is mostly in shadow, but I can see that she is looking toward the kitchen, listening intently to Mom and Dad like I am. I can only see the side of her face, but her eye is glistening; she's close to tears.

She looks like such a sad little girl that I feel sorry for her for a moment. It's hard to believe she hit a boy so hard his tooth came out.

She turns and sees me in bed, and her eyebrows go up.

"Are you sick?" She reaches over and touches my forehead like she's seen Mom and Sarah do. "Yeah, you're a little hot."

She sits silently for a couple of minutes, biting skin from around her fingernails.

"There's no point in telling anyone what really happened because no one believes anything I say," she says finally.

I want to tell her that they will believe her. Even if her teachers don't, Mom and Dad will. I'll believe her. Is she going to tell me? I look at her, hoping so much that she will.

"Dylan found out I'm in foster care, and he told everyone. He keeps being mean about it, like saying it's because my real mom hates me. He teases me till I can't take it anymore. It's so unfair. I didn't mean to hit him that hard. Blood was coming out of his mouth and everything! It was disgusting. But he shouldn't be mean all the time. It's not fair that I'm sent home and he just gets away with it."

Poor Olivia. She shouldn't have hit him, but Dylan does sound really nasty. She should have told someone when it happened instead of lashing out—but even now, if she explained, at least people would be more understanding.

"She's not upstairs!" I hear Mom calling anxiously.

"She was," Dad says, also sounding worried.

"Olivia? Olivia!"

Olivia doesn't move for a moment, but then she calls out, "I'm in here."

"She's in Jemma's room," Dad calls to Mom.

"Thank goodness," I hear Mom say. "What are you doing in there? Jemma's trying to sleep. She's not well. Come here, Olivia. Tell me what's been going on."

As Olivia leaves my room, she bursts into tears.

20

When I wake up in the morning, I am instantly aware that I don't feel feverish. I feel pleasantly cool, and it is such a relief. Dad comes in. I've been turned to face the window. He draws the curtains, and I am pleased to see that the color has returned to his face—a nice rosy pinkness.

"Sounds like you had quite a day yesterday," he says. He eases me into a sitting position with his firm, careful hands and cradles me to keep me upright, his arm around my shoulder, comfortingly.

"Sounds like you did too," I want to say.

Sarah comes in, and Dad explains that she'll have two at home today because I'm not well and Olivia is suspended.

"Maybe Olivia could read to Jemma," he says.

"Do you want to talk about what happened with Dylan?" Sarah asks Olivia as we sit in the living room later. "Your mom says you haven't told her anything."

"No, thanks," says Olivia.

"Why don't you read to Jemma?" Sarah suggests half-heartedly. She's been trying, and failing, to keep Olivia occupied all morning.

"No, can I watch something?" says Olivia. "I'm sure Jemma wants to watch something too."

"Being suspended is meant to be a punishment—not a chance to watch TV all day," Sarah tells her. "Really, I should have you scrubbing the floors or give you some math homework to do."

"No, please—not that!" Olivia has a look of horror on her face, and Sarah grins.

So she reads to me. Her school reading book is about a pony with magic powers. She holds it so I can see the words. I can read, but my eyes flicker a lot so it is hard to look at a page of text. My eyes get tired quickly too. Olivia struggles a little with reading, and I doubt she is as good as most nine-year-olds. The book seems babyish for her.

"Terrific, Olivia!" Sarah tells her when she's finished two tedious chapters. "If you had a magic pony like that, what would you do?"

"I'd ride around the world on him and get him to kick all the bad people with his superhooves—kick them until they're dead!"

I snort. Sarah's eyes widen, and I can see she's trying not to laugh as well. "Oh, Olivia! How would you know who the bad people were?"

"I just would," Olivia says, closing the book with a *snap*.

Sarah's phone beeps.

"Is that Dan?" Olivia asks, boldly trying to see over Sarah's shoulder as she pulls out the phone.

"Don't be so nosy!" Sarah gives her a nudge.

"Who is it, then?"

Sarah sighs. "Actually, it's about a gig I'm going to tomorrow night. Have you heard of Glowlight?"

"You're going to see a band?" Olivia says. "Cool... Can I come too?"

"No, it's not for kids," says Sarah. "I'll play you some of their songs if you like."

"Yeah!" Olivia jumps up, tossing the book onto the sofa.

Sarah finds a song, and the intro starts playing out of her phone.

I sing the words to myself inside my head as Sarah and Olivia bop around the living room. I love Glowlight and wish Sarah would play their music more often.

Mom comes in while we're having lunch. She plops the mail down on the kitchen table and looks briefly through the pile.

"Two for you, Jemma. You're popular today!"

"Why aren't there any for me?" Olivia demands. "No one ever writes to me."

"Most of the mail that comes is very boring, Olivia," Mom points out. "Jemma's letters are mainly hospital appointments.

This looks like one here." She tears it open. "Ah, it's from Professor Spalding."

I wait impatiently while Mom reads the letter and I try to read her expression.

"Good news and bad news, Jemma," Mom says. "Mr. Katz, the guy from Israel, would like to meet you when he's here for a conference—but it's not until July."

July is five months away! It feels like forever.

"I'll read you the other letter later," she says, tapping it gently.

My head buzzes. That must mean it's from Jodi, but Mom doesn't want to read it in front of the others. I can't wait to hear what Jodi says. But Mom said we should wait to see if I can communicate before we meet. Is she really going to make me wait five months? And then whatever they have planned may not even work anyway...

"So what have you been up to?" Mom asks Olivia as she makes herself a sandwich.

"Sarah turned on her music, and we've been dancing for hours," Olivia tells Mom.

Mom frowns at Sarah and then turns to Olivia. "I'm not sure you should be having so much fun when you've been suspended," she tells her.

"She did read to Jemma," Sarah says defensively, "and Jemma enjoyed watching her dance."

Every time I think Sarah and Mom are getting along better, they start snapping at each other again.

"I've been to your school this morning," Mom tells Olivia. "Your teacher has given me some work for you to do, so that should keep you busy this afternoon."

"Bo-ring!" groans Olivia.

When lunch is over, Mom leaves Sarah to help Olivia with her schoolwork and pushes my wheelchair into the living room. She sits close to me on the sofa and reads me my letter from Jodi.

Jodi sounds so chatty and nice. She tells me how she went out for pizza with her boyfriend and he knocked his drink over and it went all over the pizza so it was a soggy mess! And how her team won their last three field hockey matches and might win the championship. She says Mom sent a photo of me, and she can see our hair is the same color. Again, she is asking to meet me.

"Jemma." Mom sighs, looking up at me. "I really thought it would be better to wait for you to meet Mr. Katz and try his communication system before you met Jodi. But that means such a long wait for both of you. I'll talk to your dad, see what he thinks." My heart is racing. I'm sure Dad will agree. I'm sure both of them know how much this means to me.

All night, I can't stop thinking about Jodi. Over breakfast I try to figure out if Mom has spoken to Dad yet. And then, when the others have left the room, she finally says, "Jemma, I've spoken with Dad, and I've had a word with Beth too."

Beth is my social worker, and she's always eager to be helpful. I hope she agrees with Mom.

"Beth suggested I talk to Jodi first, so I've had a little talk with her on the phone."

Even though I know it's ridiculous, I get a twinge of jealousy that Mom got to speak to Jodi first. I wonder what she sounds like.

"I wanted to make sure she understands about you. I don't want her to put too much pressure on the meeting, for either of you."

I know that Mom is just being Mom—cautious as usual and wanting to explain everything carefully—but I wish she would hurry up and get to the point! None of this matters to me. Jodi is my sister. I have to meet her... I must.

"But Jodi sounds nice," says Mom finally. "I think you'll like her. She insists that she does understand. We've arranged for you to meet next weekend—on Sunday."

21

"Love will find a way," Sarah sings as she gets me dressed. She doesn't have the most tuneful voice, but she makes up for it with enthusiasm. I'm still reveling in the news about meeting Jodi next weekend, and I love the Glowlight song that Sarah is singing. The concert is tonight, and she's extra smiley, clearly excited.

She wheels me out of my room for breakfast, and something rustles beneath my wheels. Sarah gasps.

"Oh, Finn!" she says.

She turns me sideways so I can see that the hall floor is lined with neatly torn strips of newspaper, carefully arranged in rows. Finn is at the other end of the hall but comes back swiftly, looking annoyed that my wheels have moved a few strips out of place.

Dad comes downstairs. "Finn!" he exclaims. "I hope that's not today's paper. I haven't read it yet!"

The little strip near to my wheel with *Sat* on it gives him his answer. The paper is Dad's weekend treat—he doesn't have time to read one during the week. In fact, he often doesn't end up reading it on the weekend either, but I think he likes it being there. Dad looks annoyed for a second, then laughs and Sarah joins in.

Then, when Mom goes to sit down at the table for a coffee, she jumps back up again, shouting "Oww!" and clutching her bottom. From the chair, she picks up the spiky plant. Finn must have had enough of it. I bet he's moved the china elephant back to its normal spot too. The plant is squashed and misshapen, and I think Finn and I are both glad when Mom throws it in the trash.

Sarah is getting all glammed up for the concert. She paints her nails with gold nail polish. Then she does mine. It isn't easy as my hands like to curl up and my fingers are reluctant to stay straight. Muscle spasms make my arms and hands move about sometimes too. But Sarah is patient.

"Try to keep them still until they dry," she tells me. No amount of effort will give me control of my limb movements, but somehow my nails dry without too much smearing. I like the way the glint of gold catches my eye every time my head or hands move.

Now Sarah is doing her makeup. I watch as she carefully applies gold eye shadow, black eyeliner, and black mascara.

"I'll do yours in a minute," she tells me.

She looks so glamorous—like a model. She hardly ever

wears any makeup except on dates. I wonder what I will look like with makeup on.

Sarah carefully applies foundation to my skin with a sponge. It feels soft and cool.

"I'm not sure it's quite your color, but it's close enough," she says, turning me toward the mirror.

She looks at my eyes, thoughtfully. I soon have a sparkle of gold eye shadow above my eyes. The mascara is a disaster, though, as I jolt and end up with smears of black on my cheek. As Sarah rubs at it, I look like I have a black eye.

"If your mom came in now, she'd think I'd been beating you up!" says Sarah. There is an edge to her voice despite the jokey tone.

The mascara cleaned off, Sarah starts again with more foundation. I wonder if she'll bother with mascara, but she does.

"Your eyelashes are longer than mine," she says jealously.

I feel the soft grease of the lipstick as it brushes my lips.

"Look at you now!" She moves me around so I can see myself more clearly in the mirror.

I look so different. My head is still at a funny angle, my mouth gaping and not quite symmetrical, but I look older. I wish I could look like this when I meet Jodi. I look like someone about to head off to a Glowlight concert. I wish I was. I wish so much!

Sarah leaves me in the living room with the TV on while she finishes getting ready.

Dad comes in, on his way up to read bedtime stories to Finn and Olivia.

I hope he'll say something nice about my makeup, but he doesn't even notice! Now I know how Mom feels whenever she gets her hair cut. Sometimes she says she's tempted to shave her head, just to see if he realizes.

"You like Glowlight, don't you?" he says. "I'll put some on for you."

He turns off the TV, and soon the sound of Glowlight fills the room, the song with the cool drum intro at the start. Mom calls to him to turn it down.

"We like it loud, don't we, Jemma?" says Dad. "But we'd better keep your mom happy." He smiles at me and then looks closer. "Jemma! Is that makeup? You look great!"

I love the music. I absorb it—every note, every beat. I imagine I am there, with Sarah. My eyes close. Maybe this is better than really being there because in my mind I can clap and dance. I'm not in a wheelchair. I am just like everyone else.

The image of the band goes in and out of focus, and the figures around me start to blur. The notes suddenly go off-key. I look down and see my wheelchair. I'm not dancing. And then the person in front of me turns around. A face looms closer.

"If I were you, I'd kill myself." Dan's menacing grin. His cold eyes.

"I know you can't, so I've come to give you a hand to put you out of your misery."

Then I feel my chair being pushed. *I need Sarah!*

Where is she? I can't see her.

I wake with a start.

Mom is standing over me, frowning. I'm breathing fast, but my breaths come slower as I take in that it was just a bad dream, that I'd nodded off.

"What has she done to you?" Mom exclaims. "All that makeup!"

Sarah comes in. I get a wonderful whiff of her perfume.

Mom takes Sarah to one side and speaks quietly to her. I try to hear what they're saying. Sounds like Mom's complaining about my makeup, saying it will take forever to clean off.

I wish I could tell Mom I enjoyed being made up and to lay off Sarah for once.

"Enjoy the concert," Mom tells her.

"Thanks... Bye." There is still frostiness in Sarah's voice. She turns to me and smiles. "Bye, Jemma! I'll tell you all about it tomorrow!"

I hear the front door close. She's gone.

22

In the morning, Mom gets me ready.

"Looks like Sarah's sleeping in," she tells me. "Must have been a late one. I didn't even hear her come in."

I realize I didn't hear her either, though I have a blurry memory of hearing a car outside.

At about ten thirty, Olivia comes running down. "Sarah's not here! She's not in her room!"

"You shouldn't have gone in," Dad scolds her. He goes up to look and comes back confirming Olivia is right.

"Told you." Olivia pouts.

"She must be staying with one of the friends she went with to the concert," says Mom.

"She could have let us know." Dad sounds irritated. "I'll text her, just to make sure she's okay."

He does, but an hour later, he's had no reply. "Probably still asleep," he says.

I'm trying not to panic, but I don't believe Sarah has gone

back to Richard's. She sounded really certain when she said she doesn't want to be with him anymore, so why would she?

Could Dan have found out about Richard, found out that Sarah was going to the concert with him? I feel like my worst fears are coming true.

Hours go by. I keep wishing Sarah would walk through the door, bubbly, pretending not to be hungover, full of what a great concert it was.

She doesn't.

Mom tries phoning Sarah but says her phone seems to be switched off. "She probably turned it off for the concert and forgot to put it on again," says Mom. "Or left her charger at home."

By 4:00 p.m. Mom and Dad are both looking anxious. "I don't even know who she was going with," Mom comments. "Was it Dan? Do you think we should try to call him? Or her friends...that Rihanna? Who's the other one—Emma, isn't it? But how would we get hold of them? All their numbers will be in Sarah's phone."

"Should we call the police?" says Dad.

"Let's give it a few more hours," says Mom. "She's probably still hungover at Dan's or a friend's house, something like that."

Mom doesn't sound sure that she believes what she's saying, even as she says it. I am even less sure.

A few more hours go by. Mom says she'll try looking at Sarah's laptop—see if she can find a number for Dan or one of her friends—but she comes down saying she can't get into anything without Sarah's password. She finds the phone number for Sarah's sister, Kate, which Sarah gave her for emergencies. Dad phones Kate after dinner, but there's no answer. Then he phones the police.

"They took the details, but they didn't sound that interested," he tells Mom. "She's an adult. It's not like when we lost Finn."

"It isn't like her to go off and say nothing, though," says Mom.

"I did tell them that," says Dad. "I'll keep trying Kate. Sarah doesn't have any other family, does she?"

"No, her mom died years ago," says Mom. "I don't think there was anyone else."

I'm facing toward the doorway, and I can picture Sarah coming through, smiling and laughing. Then I see her at the concert, like she was in my dream. But as I try to fix the image of her in my mind, it fades. *What happened, Sarah? Where are you? Did you get to the concert? Did Dan find out? Just come home, Sarah. Please.*

23

I wake with a moment's calm on Monday, and then my stomach drops when I remember that Sarah is missing. She's still not back. This is seriously worrying. And the police aren't even looking for her yet.

Mom gets me ready. She is gentle, but her face is weary, her eyes droopy. I don't think she's had much sleep.

The glint of my sparkling nails keeps catching my eye. It feels like it was just moments ago that Sarah was putting the polish on me.

"Don't worry, Jemma. I'm sure Sarah will be home soon," Mom tells me.

It doesn't feel right for me to head off to school and act like everything is normal. Olivia doesn't want to go either. She tries hiding the car keys, but when Mom quickly finds them, she starts screaming.

"Dylan will kill me for breaking his tooth!" she yells.

"If you're worried about anything, tell a teacher," Mom

says. "I'll come in with you and explain about Sarah. I'll tell them today is a difficult day for you."

"I'm not going! I'm not going!" Olivia cries.

The bus is here to pick me up. I am wheeled out, leaving Olivia still in a tantrum.

We drive away from the house, but the same series of images runs through my mind. The frosty look Sarah gave Mom. The front door slamming as she left. Sarah at the concert, blurry figures around her. Is one of them Dan? Sarah and Richard—he's thrilled to be with her; she's worrying Dan will call. Sarah and Dan, him begging her to live with him. Sarah's phone beeping, always with Dan's name.

A new thought hits me. Could she have planned this? Could she have run away with Dan?

The next image is Dan's sneering face as he watched Ryan's funeral on TV and told me no one would catch him. If she has run away with him, she's not safe.

At school, I have swimming. It's a pain being changed and dried and changed back again, but it is always worth it. I am held in the water by Sheralyn, my volunteer helper, with the aid of some floats.

My arms and legs stretch out in the water. I feel free floating and uncurling as if I'm moving through air. In my chair I feel heavy and unwieldy; it's hard for people to move me. In water, a nudge is enough. I am as light as air, and nothing presses into me at awkward angles. The water is so soft—softer even than my bed and so gentle. It feels delicious, the strongest sensation I experience apart from eating, and far more pleasurable.

I lie on my back in the pool and stare up at the paneled ceiling. I can see my reflection repeated in a number of mirrored tiles all at once as if there are three or four of me. The mirror reflects reality, but not quite. That is how things feel with Sarah—real, but not quite. She can't really have disappeared, can she?

The water is warm, but I get cold quickly. Sheralyn comments that my fingers are going white. It is time to come out. I like Sheralyn. She is very gentle. She's training to be a teacher and says she wants to teach "people like me." She's good, but she sometimes forgets to talk to me. Sometimes while they are changing us, the volunteers start chatting to each other and forget that we are people who need to be talked to as well.

On the way home from school in the bus, I try to picture Sarah sitting in the living room. Running into the hall when I come through the door. I pray, even though I don't know if I believe in God.

"Please, God," I say in my head, "please let Sarah be home." She is not.

Later, after dinner, Mom is putting Finn and Olivia to bed, and I'm keeping Dad company in the kitchen while he does the dishes. The phone rings, and he quickly dries his hands on a towel and grabs it.

I hold my breath. My heartbeat thuds in my ears. "Oh, hello, Kate," says Dad. "You got my message?"

Maybe Kate knows something. Maybe Sarah is with her. I listen eagerly, but Dad takes the phone out of the room.

Mom comes running down the stairs. "Who is it?" she says. "Any news?"

"Kate just saw the message now," says Dad as they both come back into the kitchen. "She's not spoken to Sarah for about a month, but that's not unusual. They're not that close. She didn't sound too worried, though. She said Sarah's sometimes a little impulsive. She went missing for a few days when she was a teenager. She'd gone off with some boy she liked and didn't bother to tell anyone."

"She's not a teenager now, though," Mom says doubtfully. "She's a woman in her twenties with a job and responsibilities. If she wanted to go off with Dan, why wouldn't she just tell us? What do you think, Ben?"

Dad shrugs. "It's hard to believe she'd go and leave all her stuff here."

"Go where?" Olivia has appeared in the doorway in her nightie. "You're talking about Sarah, aren't you? Where's she gone? Tell me."

"Bedtime, Olivia," says Dad. "We're sure Sarah will be back soon."

24

Sarah's been missing for three days. Mom and Dad are talking a lot in hushed whispers.

"Kate suggested we try her laptop again. She gave a few suggestions for passwords," Dad tells Mom.

"I'll try," says Mom. "One of her friends must know where she is."

The one person they need to contact is the one they won't even think of looking for. They need to speak to Richard.

Dad puts on a Disney movie for us when we're all back from school. I don't feel like watching it. I want to do something. I want to help find Sarah.

Mom spends a while in Sarah's room. She comes down sighing.

"I checked and I'm sure all her stuff is still there, like we thought—her iPad, her clothes, her jewelry," Mom says. "I tried a few passwords for the laptop, and would you believe it was 'Jemma' and her birth date?"

I am Sarah's password! I get a painful ache in my chest. I wish they'd realize that I am also the real-life password to the information they need.

"Good job!" says Dad, impressed.

"I searched her contacts and Facebook friends, but I can't see Dan there, which is strange. She doesn't use email much," Mom tells Dad. "I guess it's all texts these days. But she'd sent messages to Rihanna and Emma. I've emailed both of them to see if they were with her on Saturday or if they know how to get in touch with Dan. The emails don't mention the concert, but one to Rihanna mentions what a bitch I've been to her lately." Mom's voice cracks slightly. "I know we haven't been getting along very well. But things weren't bad enough for her to walk out on us, though."

"I don't think so," says Dad.

I think about Dan trying to convince Sarah to leave me. She was tempted, I'm sure. She wasn't as happy here as she used to be.

The police arrive just after dinner. Two officers walk into the kitchen. They are both tall and with their uniforms, the kitchen seems instantly too full. I see the man glance at me and then quickly look away, while the woman smiles as if she's ignoring the tense atmosphere. It's like the room itself is holding its breath.

"I'll put the television on for the children," Mom tells them. I wonder if I am going to be sent off to the living room with Finn and Olivia.

"Have you found Sarah?" Olivia asks the policewoman.

She shakes her head. "We're trying our best," she says, and then introduces herself to us as Officer Sahin.

"You should look harder," Olivia tells them. "Dad found Finn with some chocolate chip cookies. Maybe if we get something that Sarah really likes, that'll make her come back. I know! She loves Glowlight. Maybe if we put their music on—or maybe we can even get the band to come here and put an announcement on the TV. She won't want to miss that."

"Thanks for your help," Officer Sahin says, smiling. "It's nice to hear your ideas."

"So will you do it, then?" Olivia demands.

"Come on, Olivia," says Mom.

Olivia hesitates. She'd love to stay, just as I would, but she loves TV too and follows Mom. Finn goes with them. The police officers sit down at the kitchen table. They smile at me, but seem unsure whether to speak to me.

"You must be worried about your aide," says Officer Sahin.

I certainly am. My head jolts back, and an *ughhh* noise comes out of me.

"Is she compos mentis?" the man, Officer Hunt, asks Mom quietly as she comes back in.

"Oh yes, but she can't communicate. I wish she could. Sarah talks to her a lot."

"Not much use to us, then," Officer Hunt mutters, screwing up his nose.

I wish I could kick him.

Mom looks at me and then makes coffee for the police officers. She leaves me where I am. She's decided I should be in on this, maybe because Sarah is my aide or maybe she feels bad about what the policeman just said.

Officer Hunt starts asking Mom questions. It's all background stuff—how long Sarah has been here, how the care is paid for. I have a question of my own: How is this going to help find her? Mom tells them about Dan, that she's been trying to get ahold of him.

Finally, Officer Hunt begins asking questions about the night Sarah went missing. But of course all Mom knows is that Sarah was going to the concert. She doesn't know who with; she doesn't think it was Dan. Emma and Rihanna replied to Mom's email, but they didn't know about the concert and haven't heard from Sarah either. They also didn't know much about Dan.

"Most missing people reappear within forty-eight hours," Officer Sahin tells Mom. "Now that three days have passed, this is, of course, more concerning, but please try not to worry. We will pass the details to the Missing Persons Bureau, but we have classified her as 'low risk.' The most likely thing is still that she has gone off of her own accord, that she's with her boyfriend or some other friends."

"I really don't know," says Mom. "Dan seems like a good person to me. I don't see why they'd go off together without telling us."

"We will try to trace Sarah's phone," says Officer Hunt, "and also speak to Dan. It's a shame no one knows his last name."

It seems odd to me that he isn't on Facebook and Sarah's friends don't know him.

The doorbell rings while the police are still talking, through.

Mom goes to get the door, leaving the kitchen in silence. I recognize the voice, even though I've only met him a few times. It's Richard. Is Sarah with him?

"Is Sarah in?" I hear him ask Mom.

"Oh...Richard," says Mom. "No, she's not—"

"Her phone's been off since the concert," Richard interrupts. "I'm kind of worried that she's not been in touch. Maybe I did something to upset her."

"She went to the concert with you?" says Mom.

"Yes! Who did you think she went with?" says Richard. Then he pauses. "Wh-what's wrong?"

Mom lowers her voice as she explains to him what's happened. I can't hear his reaction, but the next moment Richard comes into the kitchen, blinking likes someone who's come into a bright room from somewhere dark.

He looks from Officer Hunt to Officer Sahin and back at Mom. He shifts around on his feet. Then he glances back toward the front door as if he wishes he could make a fast getaway.

Mom explains to the police about Richard being with Sarah at the concert. Richard begins to babble.

"We met downtown, went to the concert, and afterward I drove Sarah back here. She got out of the car, and I watched her walk up the sidewalk to the front door. She had her key out. I didn't wait for her to go inside. I drove off. Oh my God! How could something happen to her at the front door?"

"Do you remember what time you dropped her off?" Officer Hunt asks him.

"Let me think. It must have been about eleven thirty."

"Are you sure she didn't come in and then go out again?" Officer Sahin asks Mom.

"I didn't hear the door, and it doesn't look like she changed clothes or anything. I really don't think so."

I know she didn't. I'd have heard the front door. But what Richard is saying sounds so unlikely—he brought her back, and she *disappeared* before coming inside. Can that really be true?

Officer Sahin turns to Richard. "And you didn't have any kind of a fight? She wasn't upset?"

"No, we had a great time. She's always smiling, Sarah. I don't think I've seen her upset in the ten months we've been going out! We've never fought... I can tell you that."

I see Mom's eyebrows shoot up to her hairline. Her mouth drops open. She's not sure what to say. As far as she's concerned, they broke up three months ago, when Sarah started going out with Dan.

Officer Hunt turns to Mom. "I thought you said her boyfriend was named Dan."

"Dan?" Richard repeats. "Who's Dan?"

Mom's hand covers her eyes as if she wishes she could hide. She slowly takes a breath and then looks at Richard.

Richard's mouth is taut as Mom explains about Dan. His eyes are still, staring at her and then at the wall. "I don't believe it... I don't believe it." His eyes are glassy now.

He's being so dramatic that I begin to wonder if he knew already.

I'd been worrying so much that Dan would find out about Richard, but what if Richard found out about Dan? Does that change things?

"You appear to be the last person who saw her," says Officer Sahin.

25

There is still no news about Sarah. Four days. That's double the time they said missing people usually turn up in.

Finn is doing his head-banging thing more and more, and Olivia is having even more tantrums than usual. Mom's put the TV on for them, and they're quiet for the time being, watching a kids' show about aliens. I'm in the kitchen keeping Mom company while she cooks dinner. She seems to like having me close to her at the moment. I don't think she likes being alone. Or maybe she's worried about how I'm feeling without Sarah.

Someone rings the doorbell, and Mom hurries to open the door. I hear Paula's voice.

"Lorraine! I heard about Sarah. The police came to speak to us. What do you think has happened to her?"

"Come in, Paula," Mom says. "Have a cup of tea." As she leads Paula into the kitchen, Mom catches my eye with a look that says she could have done without Paula turning up.

"The police think she's gone off somewhere of her own accord," Mom says, pulling out a chair.

Paula sits down.

"You don't mind if I continue?" Mom asks, pointing to the chopping board full of waiting carrots.

"They said that when I first reported Ryan missing," says Paula. Mom stares at her and then glances at me.

But Paula doesn't seem to take the hint. "I said to Graham, it's strange that the police should come to us. Only a few doors apart. And so soon after my Ryan..."

There's a loud snap as Mom chops a carrot with extra force. I see her breathe in and compose herself. "Paula, I'm not sure what you're—"

"Do you think they're linked? It can't just be a coincidence."

Paula gives me an awkward glance. She's clearly wondering if she should be saying all this in front of me. I swallow. I want her to keep talking. Even though what she's implying has happened to Sarah is making my chest hurt, I want them to realize there is a connection—Dan and Sarah, Dan and Ryan. Dan.

But looking from Mom to Paula, my heart sinks. The desperation in Paula's eyes. Mom will just think it's Paula's grief, that she's trying to make things fit together so she can have an answer.

"They're speaking to everyone who lives on this block,"

Mom says softly but firmly. "Richard says Sarah got out of his car just outside the house around eleven thirty on Saturday night. The police want to know if anyone heard or saw anything."

"Yes," says Paula. "That's what they asked us. But we both take sleeping pills, you see. Don't get a wink otherwise—not since...you know. Do you really think she just took off?"

"I don't know what to think," says Mom. She pours tea for Paula and then goes back to chopping the carrots loudly. "Have you gotten any news yourselves, about Ryan?"

Paula sighs deeply and runs her finger around the rim of her mug. "Nothing," she says. "I got my hopes up when they charged that Jay. He was Ryan's regular dealer, and they had a falling-out about money or something. But Jay was out of town—he proved it. The more time that goes by, the less likely I think it is that they'll get him." She looks up. "Though perhaps now..." The doorbell rings again.

"Goodness, we're popular tonight!" Mom exclaims. She turns down the heat under a pan on the stove and excuses herself. The smell of hamburger frying wafts over me as she goes out into the hall.

Paula meets my eyes briefly for a moment and looks as if she might say something, but then thinks better of it. People do that a lot.

Mom's voice is loud with surprise as she opens the front door.

"Oh, Dan..." I hear her say.

26

I can't believe he's here. I feel suddenly cold, so cold. Mom is talking to him as he follows her into the kitchen. "We wanted to call you," she's saying, "but we couldn't find your number."

"Call me? Why? Has something happened?" Dan asks as he comes into the room. "I—" He stops when he sees Paula. He doesn't look at me at all.

"Paula, this is Dan, Sarah's boyfriend," says Mom. She runs her hand across her forehead. Her eyes are wide with shock. If Dan's here, that means Sarah hasn't run off with him.

Paula nods.

"Dan, this is my neighbor, Paula," Mom continues. Dan nods back. Does he realize who Paula is?

"What's going on?" he asks. "Sarah's phone has been off. I came over to see her."

"Oh, Dan," says Mom, her voice shaking. "She isn't here. We haven't seen her since Saturday. Haven't you heard from her at all?"

"No. What's going on?"

Dan turns his head to look at Mom, and I can't see his face. I wish I could. I bet his expression would give him away.

Paula stands up, her chair scraping the floor noisily in her haste. "I'd better be going," she says. "I do hope she turns up."

"Turns up?" Dan repeats. He looks at Paula, and I see a crease spread across his forehead. I watch him closely. He definitely looks surprised to hear that Sarah is missing. There are beads of sweat on his forehead. Does he really know nothing, or is this all an act?

"I'll see Paula to the door, then I'll tell you everything, Dan," Mom says.

For a moment I am alone with Dan. I wish he'd say something, confide in me. I watch him. His hands don't keep still. He's rubbing his fingers together.

Mom is back. Phlegm clogs my throat, and I cough.

"Dan, the police have been looking for you," Mom tells him.

He seems nervous now, his feet shifting back and forth. His eyes flash in alarm. "What? Why?" he asks.

"You haven't seen or heard from her then, Dan—not since Saturday? We thought she might have been with you."

Dan shakes his head. "No."

"Sarah was at a concert on Saturday night and didn't come back here. No one's seen her since. Sit down, Dan—this must be a shock. I'll make you coffee."

Dan moves toward a chair and leans on the back of it, but he doesn't sit down. "A concert? I thought she was working last weekend."

It's Mom's turn to shift around awkwardly.

I look at Dan. I'm sure this is an act. He's challenging Mom to confirm what he knows—that Sarah was two-timing him.

"She went with a friend...actually, her ex, Richard. I think he must have gotten tickets for the concert a long time ago. She probably felt she had to go. You know what she's like!"

"Right," says Dan, with an edge to his voice. "So I assume the police have been questioning him?"

"Yes," Mom says. "He was the last person to see her, but I don't think they... They want to speak to you too. You'll call them, won't you?"

Dan's gaze is steady. "Of course," he says.

27

I spend all the next day wondering what will happen when Dan talks to the police. He has to call them, doesn't he? But one thing we know now is that Sarah hasn't run off with him. Could she have left on her own? Would she really do that? Or has something else happened, something I can't stand to even think about?

When I get home from school, I'm surprised to find Sheralyn, my swimming volunteer, waiting for me. Mom says when she told the principal at my school what had happened, she said Sheralyn might be able to help out because she's worked as an aide before. It turns out she's still registered with the agency Mom uses, and she was eager to help. I'm glad it's Sheralyn, but at the same time, having her here only makes me want Sarah back more, if that's possible. Sarah has been missing for five days.

Sheralyn decides to take me for a walk to the shopping center. Maybe she's trying to take my mind off things, but

I hate the place. Too many people staring. They either look appalled or desperately sorry for me. There's always some kid with a finger up one nose pointing at me with the other hand and saying, "What's wrong with her?" Sarah used to bring me here a lot, but I think she sensed all the comments were upsetting me and we stopped coming so often.

As we reach the center, I recognize a man who is walking toward us. It's Dan's friend Billy. I see him look and recognize me, but he just walks straight past. It's the total opposite of what he was like before. Of course, he doesn't know Sheralyn, but would it hurt to stop and say hello?

As we reach the more crowded shopping area, I start thinking about my sister. She doesn't live that far away. What if she was here now, walking around the stores? I wonder if I would recognize her from the photo. I'm looking at every girl and wondering if she could be her. That girl with dark hair looks too tall. This one has a kind face, but her hair is too light.

Ahead there is a woman with blond hair, tied back in a ponytail, walking away from us. My heart suddenly skips a beat. *Sarah.* She looks like Sarah. She really could be... She could be Sarah! She's walking faster than us. She's disappearing into the crowd. *Wait!*

She doesn't wait. She's gone. It couldn't have been Sarah, could it? If she's run away, she wouldn't still be around here. She'd be worried about being spotted. I don't think she walked quite like Sarah either. I have a lingering hope, though. Maybe it was her. Maybe she's on her way home. Perhaps she's stopped at the store to buy some flowers—or something to give Mom, to give all of us, to say sorry for all the worry she's caused.

She doesn't need to say *sorry* to me. I'd forgive her for getting us all so worried if she only came home.

"Hey—wait!" a woman calls. Sheralyn stops and swings me around. The woman has short gray hair. She must be sixty or seventy. What does she want?

"Here, take this for the poor lass," the woman says.

She holds out a ten-dollar bill.

I can't see Sheralyn's face, as she is pushing me, but I hear the shock in her voice.

"No... Really, that's very kind, but—"

"Please, dear," says the woman. "I insist. Take it." The money has gone from the woman's hand.

I'm not a charity. Sarah would never have done that. She would have explained that I am well looked after, that I have what I need. I don't need strangers giving me money in the street. I'm not a desperate homeless person.

"Sorry, Jemma," Sheralyn says quietly as the woman disappears in the crowd. "That was so embarrassing. I didn't know what to say. I'll donate the money to charity."

When we get back, I am still feeling upset about the woman treating me like a charity case. Mom's upstairs with

Finn and Olivia, but Sheralyn takes over with them and Mom comes down. She's holding something—a letter!

"Jemma, I've got another letter for you from Jodi," she says.

I can feel my heart beating faster as Mom begins to read.

Dear Jemma,

This is just a short note to say I am so excited about meeting you on Sunday! I can't wait, and I can't think about anything else! Your mom was so great on the phone. She's told me all about you. I hope you are as excited as I am! I'm counting the days and the hours and the minutes!

Love, Jodi

Mom folds the letter and looks at me.

"Jemma, I'd forgotten we arranged this. I wonder if we should postpone it."

"No!" I want to yell. I know everything with Sarah is awful, but I want to meet Jodi so much. I need something good to happen, and this is going to be it. I must meet my sister.

"Then again," says Mom, "we don't want to let Jodi down. This is such a big deal for both of you. Maybe it will take your mind off things."

Mom sighs. I'm relieved. I just hope she doesn't change her mind again.

When I get back from school the next day, Olivia's already home, and she's jumping up and down with excitement. My heart races. Is it Sarah... Is she back? I've been full of excitement myself all day about meeting Jodi on Sunday, but Olivia can't be excited about that.

"Guess what?" she says, bounding up to me. "I took a photo of Sarah to school, and I showed it around to see if anyone had seen her—and Ruby Jones says she saw her in the supermarket!"

"Don't get your hopes up too high, Olivia," Mom says gently. "It was probably someone who looks like Sarah."

So Sarah is not back. I get a pang of guilt for feeling happy about meeting Jodi when Sarah is still missing.

"It was her," Olivia insists. "Ruby said she was sure!"

"It might have been Sarah that Ruby saw," Mom acknowledges. "It also might not."

"It was her," Olivia insists again.

I wish it was. I wish so much that it was Sarah who Ruby saw in the supermarket and who I saw in the shopping center.

During dinner, the phone rings. Dad answers it. "Oh, Kate! Hello," he says. "Any news? How are you coping?"

"Tell her Ruby saw Sarah," Olivia demands. "She'll want to know. You must tell her."

"Shhhh! Wait," Mom whispers. "Let's find out why she's called first."

"You have? Really?" says Dad. "Do any of them seem likely?"

Likely? What could that mean?

I can't see Dad's face, but I can see how eagerly Mom and Olivia are watching him. Finn is tapping his fork on his plate. *Tap, tap, tap*, over and over.

I wish he'd stop.

Dad says something about a card. And then "That's typical."

"What's she saying?" Olivia demands. "Have they found Sarah or what? Tell her about Ruby. Ruby saw her!"

"Shhhh!" Mom tells her, putting her finger to her lips.

"That sounds like an excellent idea," Dad continues after listening for a few moments. "Of course we'll help in any way we can. Just let us know."

He puts the phone down. Mom looks at him questioningly.

"Why didn't you tell her?" Olivia shouts. She stands up and kicks her chair over.

"Stop that, Olivia!" Dad says firmly. "Sit down and listen if you want to know what Kate said."

Olivia hesitates, but she does want to know. She picks up her chair and sits down.

"Kate's started a social media campaign, and she's already had a few people contact her with sightings," Dad tells Mom.

"See? I told you Ruby saw her!" Olivia interrupts. "I told you, and you didn't believe it."

"The first few didn't sound likely," Dad continues, "but

now there've been three quite close together—all within ten miles of here—that do sound possible. The most interesting news is that the police say Sarah's debit card was used two days ago to withdraw a hundred dollars—and the ATM is in Watford, not far from those three sightings."

Sarah has taken money from an ATM. That must mean she's alive, doesn't it? Or is this Dan trying to throw people off the scent?

"Goodness," says Mom. "Was there a security camera at the ATM?"

"The camera near it wasn't working, and they couldn't see anyone matching her description on the other nearby cameras—though they're still going through the footage. The police think it's a good sign. Her phone was last used at the concert itself, so that hasn't been much help. Kate is certainly hopeful, though."

"It was her," says Olivia firmly.

"Kate's put Sarah's details on the Missing People web page. If someone doesn't want to be found, they can still leave a message on there, just so family and friends know they are okay. Kate is getting some posters made, and she's asked if we'll help put them up around here."

"I'll help!" says Olivia.

If Sarah has been seen, if she's used an ATM, then it truly sounds possible she chose to leave. I want her to be alive, even though it's hard to bear the thought that she left us like that—that she was so unhappy. I can't take this much longer, this limbo.

Later, Mom gets out the nail-polish remover and takes off my now-chipped nail polish. I keep thinking about Sarah putting it on me so carefully, so kindly. I can see her sparkly eyes, her excitement about the concert. I don't want Mom to take it off. It connects me to Sarah, and, without it, I feel like Sarah is even farther away. But soon the nail polish has gone and only the strong smell of the remover lingers, making me cough. I wonder if anyone will ever paint my nails again.

28

It is a week since Sarah went missing. *A whole week*.

Kate has come with a stack of posters, and we are going around the streets putting them up. I've never met Kate before. She doesn't look like Sarah. She is much shorter, and her face is narrower. Her hair is dark, and Sarah's is fair. She has lines on her face. She looks much older than Sarah.

"Hi, Jemma, nice to meet you," she says, smiling a little awkwardly. I jolt at the way she speaks. Her voice is so similar it could be Sarah's.

Dad wasn't sure about all of us coming, but Olivia was determined to help.

I am "parked" in front of a streetlight where the first poster has been attached. It is weird seeing Sarah's face smiling down. Is she smiling somewhere now? I can't picture what she's doing, where she might be. It's just a blank. Kate seems so confident that the sightings were really Sarah and that she's alive. Could it be true? Could it?

Dad asks Kate if the police have followed up on the sightings and the ATM.

"They're still not sure if it was her," Kate admits, "but there's no proof that it wasn't either."

"And Ruby Jones saw her too!" Olivia pipes up.

"Yes, so you said," says Kate. "Any sighting might help. It's good that she told you."

Once the posters are up, I am disappointed to see most people going past without even looking at them. If they look at all, it is such a quick glance that they can't really take in her face—can they?

Sheralyn is with me and is supposed to be watching Finn too. To make him feel useful, Dad has given him a wad of posters to hold, while Olivia is handing Dad pieces of tape. Sheralyn is watching Olivia. No one apart from me has noticed that Finn is now lining up his posters neatly on the sidewalk against the fence. He has more than I thought—at least ten faces of Sarah staring up from the ground—and I can see what's going to happen. It's not that windy, but it will only take a little bit of a breeze. *Please, Sheralyn... Look back! Look at Finn!*

She does—but too late. A gust lifts the corner of one sheet, then another, and suddenly they are all fluttering up into the air, spreading across the sidewalk.

Finn lets out an anguished cry and starts flapping his arms, his neat work undone.

"Oh! Finn!" Sheralyn exclaims.

He makes no effort to pick up the posters, just watches as Sheralyn, Dad, and Olivia quickly try to gather them. Some are flapping into the street like injured birds. Olivia runs to the edge of the curb.

"Olivia—not in the street!" Dad yells, and to my relief, Olivia stops.

A car runs over a poster, and even from here, I can see tire marks on it.

"I could have gotten that one!" Olivia tells Dad angrily. Mom and Kate are farther down the street. I can't see them, but I hear Kate's voice. They must have seen and come back to help. I only see Kate when she steps into the street and retrieves the poster with the tire marks. She stands on the sidewalk in front of me, staring at it and brushing it with her hand, as if the tire marks might rub off. Tears run down her face.

As we head home, it begins to rain—just to make everyone more miserable—and no one has an umbrella. Although they are in plastic sleeves, the posters will be dripping and bedraggled before anyone even sees them. Mom and Sheralyn struggle to get my shower-proof cape over me, but I am already very wet. The chilly dampness has seeped through to my skin, making me shiver. Raindrops tickle my face like insects, and I wish I could wipe them away.

When we reach the house, Mom says Kate can't go all

that way home on the train when she's soaked through. She insists on lending her some clothes and invites Kate to stay for dinner.

Once I am in dry clothes, Sheralyn leaves me in the living room with some music playing, saying she's going to take a shower. Kate, Mom, and Dad are in the kitchen, and I wish she'd taken me in there.

I'm sitting here, almost asleep, when Olivia slips in, unusually quietly for her. She goes over to Mom's purse, which is on the sofa, opens the zipper, and starts digging in it. I wonder briefly if Mom has asked her to fetch something from her bag—but it's unlikely. Olivia keeps glancing toward the door, so she's obviously doing something she shouldn't.

She doesn't seem to have realized that I'm here. I watch as she pulls out Mom's wallet and takes out a ten-dollar bill. She folds it and presses it quickly into her pocket. She zips up Mom's bag, then glances up at me. She meets my eyes, but then looks quickly away and hurries off.

What does Olivia want ten dollars for? Then I remember Mom saying money was missing from her purse. It was Olivia all along.

———

"Sarah was a little on the wild side as a teenager. She had a string of hopeless boyfriends," Kate tells us over dinner.

"Not much change there," I want to say.

"And like I said," Kate continues, "I tried to warn her about this one boy, and she got annoyed and went off with him for a few days."

"But she hasn't gone off with Dan—or with Richard," Mom points out. "They've both been here and are clearly worried about her."

"I know," says Kate.

There's a silence, and I feel them all thinking about the other possibilities that no one wants to mention—the bad things that could have happened to Sarah.

When Kate leaves after we've eaten, I miss her voice. I miss her voice that sounds so much like Sarah's.

29

We pass one of our posters as Mom drives me to the Family Center where the meeting with Jodi has been arranged. I had imagined we'd meet in a café or something like that, but Mom says this will be more private, and Jodi will have a social worker there to support her if she needs someone to talk to afterward. Whatever I feel after this meeting will have to stay inside me. I can't share it. I hope it will go okay.

I am starting to feel sick as we go over bumps in the road. I'm relieved that it's not a long drive, and I am soon out of the car and being pushed by Mom up the ramp of a modern building that looks like a preschool.

Mom speaks to someone at the reception desk, and we are directed to the back of the building. Is Jodi here already?

We've arrived first and have to sit in a room similar to a doctor's waiting room. It's all making this feel so formal. Mom pulls me near her and squeezes my hand. I am grateful. I know she is nervous too. Then, after a few minutes, a woman with an ID on a lanyard comes bustling up to us, smiling.

"I'm Donna," she tells us. "I'm a social worker. Jodi is on her way. Would you like to come through to the room we've set up for you?"

Mom nods.

"Can I get you a coffee while you're waiting?"

"Thanks, that would be great," says Mom.

"Would you like anything, Jemma?"

"No, she's fine," says Mom. *Fine? I'm not sure about that!*

The room is cozy with armchairs and a striped rug, but the pale lime-green walls and shiny plastic floor make it still look like a doctor's exam room. There is a landscape picture on the wall of fields and farm buildings and a scarecrow. It looks like a beautiful day—the sky is so blue, and there are lots of shadows on the ground. I stare at the picture. It is calming.

"I hope she won't be long," says Mom, looking at her watch and bringing me back to now. I wish I could have stayed with the picture. I've been excited so far, but I'm suddenly feeling really shaky inside.

It is a few minutes before Donna brings the coffee.

She goes out, leaving Mom clutching the mug as if for warmth, though it's not cold in here. She's anxious too—wondering if she's done the right thing, whether this is a good idea. She couldn't change her mind now, could she?

Donna is back, smiling. "She's here! She's just stopped in the restroom. A little nervous, I think!"

"I'm sure Jemma must be nervous too," says Mom.

"You shouldn't worry, though," Donna tells me. "We won't get in the way, but we'll both be here, on hand if needed." She winks. It reminds me of Dan winking, though it is a very different wink. I'm sure this wink is saying "good luck" rather than "I'll be back to kill you sometime." It makes me slightly uneasy, though. Mom and Donna move their chairs toward the far wall so Jodi and I will have some space. I can't see them now because I'm facing the door.

Then the door opens slowly, and a girl comes in. She glances past me toward Mom, and I hear Donna say warmly, "Come on in, Jodi. This is Jemma."

Jodi walks toward me and stands still. We stare at each other. She is a prettier than her photo, with dark hair and a fluffy black sweater. The shock is—she looks far more like me than I'd realized. Our hair, dark eyes, small noses, and pale, thin lips are so similar. My face looks as if it has been squashed in sideways. It is distorted, my features out of alignment. Yet I can see myself in her. We are so alike! She is shocked too. I can see it. Her mouth has dropped slightly open.

I wish she'd speak, and I wish she'd sit down. She's standing too still for too long. I think she's frozen.

"Oh...Jemma," she says at last.

I love it. I love hearing her say my name.

My sister saying my name! I wait for more.

Her face creases up. She bursts into tears.

"I'm so sorry, Jemma. I can't do this!" she sobs.

Her hands cover her tearstained face. I hadn't noticed the makeup until now when I see it smearing down her cheeks.

I want to reassure her, to tell her to sit down, not to worry. I realize my delight in seeing the likeness between us has had the opposite effect on her. She is horrified to be so like someone so deformed. I'd normally be angry, but I can't be. I'll forgive her anything if she'll just talk to me. She's my sister. My sister.

Donna rushes over. "Jodi, why don't you sit down for a minute? I can understand this being a little overwhelming. I'll get you a tissue."

But Jodi doesn't sit.

"Jodi?" Mom tries.

"Stop crying, stop crying, please!" I want to beg her. But suddenly the door has opened and shut, and in a blur, she is gone.

30

Donna hurries after her, and a few moments later, Mom follows.

I am alone. I don't think I've ever felt as alone as in this moment. I only had a sister for about two minutes, but now there is a gaping hole in my life. She's gone. If this is what she meant about a missing piece, I understand now. I'm missing her. But I was not her missing piece. Like Mom feared, I was not what Jodi was looking for. She's had a glimpse, and I don't fit the gap in her puzzle.

I'm not alone for long, of course. Mom rushes back in and hugs me. My face is wet. I realize it is Mom crying, but when she finally lets go of me, my face gets wetter still. I am crying too.

"Donna's talking to her now," Mom says. "She might calm down and come back in, but it's possible she might not. I'm so sorry, Jemma."

We wait. Mom strokes my hand. We wait more.

I stare at the picture, the sunshine and the shadows. She

will come back. She'll calm down. Donna will talk to her. She'll come back in.

We wait...and wait. Mom looks out into the corridor. "They're still in that room," she tells me. "That has to be a good sign. You still want to see her, Jemma, don't you?" Mom looks at me closely. "Maybe we should've waited until you could communicate. It's not fair to you. It would've been easier for Jodi too."

Maybe Mom's right—but who knows how long that's going to take, and if it will ever happen. I don't want to wait for that. I want to see Jodi now. I can't stand that she's so close—across that corridor—and yet so, so far away.

Come back, Jodi! Please come back.

The door across the corridor bangs. The bang echoes down the hallway. Mom hesitates, unsure whether to go out to see what's happened or to wait. Our door opens. Donna comes in. She is alone. My heart sinks.

"I am so sorry," Donna says, her voice low and grim, the opposite of the buzzy chirp she met us with earlier. She goes on, talking about how bad Jodi feels, but I am feeling too sad to listen.

"Is she still here?" Mom asks hopefully. "Maybe I can talk to her."

Donna shakes her head, and my heart sinks down my legs and under my wheels. She's gone. It's as if she's closed the door on me.

She came, she took one look, and she went. That was my sister.

Back at home, I'm in a daze as Dad wheels me into the living room. I can see he has been playing Connect Four with Olivia while Finn lines up matchsticks along the wall. Finn is wearing a helmet because he's been head-banging so much lately. Mom tells Dad what happened with Jodi and then says she has a migraine and needs to lie down.

"I think we need to build a nest for Jemma," Dad tells Olivia.

"A nest?" Olivia asks. "What do you mean?"

"Jemma's had a hard morning and needs some TLC. We'll stack up as many cushions as we can find into a nest, and Jemma can sit in it and feel soft and safe and warm."

"Can I sit in it too?" Olivia asks.

"After Jemma's had a turn, you certainly can," says Dad.

Dad got into this "nesting" years ago when I was about five. He used to make nests for me all the time. It's been a long time since he's made me one. I thought I'd grown out of them, but the thought of him doing this for me fills me with warmth and love, and I realize I'm yearning to be snuggled and safe.

Olivia and Dad get busy with cushions.

I count as they pile them up. They get up to ten in the end. Olivia stands back as Dad eases me gently into the nest. Even Finn pauses for a moment and looks up as I am lowered into the softness.

"How's that?" Dad asks.

I am held, nestled, caressed by the comforting cushions—though I can't be left alone in it in case I roll or cushions fall over me and I can't breathe.

"Is it my turn now?" Olivia asks.

"Let Jemma have some time in it first," Dad tells her. I expect her to protest.

"She does look cozy," Olivia acknowledges. I'd smile at her if I could.

My nest is so comfy, and I can feel Dad's warmth and even Olivia's too—but I'm still so sad inside. I'm missing Sarah so much, and I want my sister to come back. I want Jodi.

———

An hour later, I am back in my wheelchair. Olivia had a turn in the nest after me. Finn showed no interest, though I think he would be in it in a shot if no one was here. Dad has gone upstairs to check on Mom.

Finn is still lining up matchsticks, while Olivia is lining up all the dolls on the top floor of her dollhouse and then knocking them one by one out the window, saying, "*Wheeeeeee! Thump*—you're dead!"

I half watch her, but not closely, because my mind is elsewhere. I am thinking about Jodi. Her face is imprinted on my mind—her likeness, the connection between us. Did Jodi feel it? Maybe she did, and it was so strong it overwhelmed her. I wonder what she's doing right now, how she's feeling.

I realize after a while that I can't see Finn or Olivia. I'm not sure if they've left the room or are out of sight behind me, but then I hear an unhappy grunting sound that must be Finn.

The sound is coming from behind me. Finn suddenly lurches past.

"Get back here," Olivia says, but Finn is wriggling toward the door. He scrambles past me, hotly pursued by Olivia. She tries to grab him, but he is out of the room in a flash. Poor Finn. I want to protect him. If I could move my legs, I'd love to give Olivia a gentle sisterly kick. If I could talk, I'd ask her what's bothering her, and maybe she'd tell me, like she told me about Dylan.

Olivia holds her head up high and struts out.

As I sit alone thinking, I start to feel achy. I hope it's just the worry making this happen and that I'm not getting sick. That's all I need.

There's a sudden piercing scream from upstairs. "What's happened?" I hear Dad demanding.

"Finn head butted me with his helmet!" Olivia screeches. "I think he's cracked my head open!" She is wailing.

Maybe Finn can stand up for himself after all.

Later in the evening when Finn and Olivia are in bed, Dad wheels me into the living room. We find Mom in there, curled up in my nest, looking cozy, eating a bar of chocolate.

31

I feel wiped out, and I don't want to go to school. The bus arrives, and Sheralyn comes with me because today is swimming.

The pool is not as warm today as it should be. I float, but I don't enjoy it. I feel shivery. Last week at swimming, Sarah had only been missing a day. I was sure she'd be back when I got home. Now I'm scared she's really not coming back. I thought with the posters and Kate's campaign and the debit card that she might be found, but there's been no more news.

Back at home, the phone rings while we are eating dinner. If the phone rang during dinner, the rule used to be that no one answered it. The person could leave a message. Now that rule is constantly broken. The phone rings much more often than it did too. Dad jumps up and answers it. "Yes," he says.

Then I see the color drain from his face as he listens. I can't swallow. It's Sarah. It has to be about Sarah. Mushed carrot sits in my mouth, and a little spills out. Sheralyn doesn't notice. She's looking at Dad. We all are—apart from Finn, who is busy trying to line up the carrot sticks on his plate.

"One minute," says Dad. He gives Mom a look and goes out into the hall with the phone.

"What's happened?" Olivia demands. "Is Sarah dead? Did someone murder her? How did they do it? Was it a knife or a gun, or did they strangle her?"

"Olivia!" Mom bellows in horror. "Be quiet!"

"I want to know!" Olivia protests.

Some mushed carrot has dripped onto my pale, cream top.

I am sure I hear Dad swear out in the hall. I don't think I've ever heard him swear before. The news must be bad.

"Ooh, yuck! Look at Jemma!" Olivia cries, screwing up her face.

Sheralyn and Mom both turn to me quickly.

"Oh... Sorry, Jemma," Sheralyn says, anxiously glancing from me to Mom, who has already jumped up to grab a kitchen towel.

"Here," Mom says, passing it to Sheralyn.

Dad comes back in. He looks pale, and his eyes look deeper than usual and darker.

"What's happened?" Olivia demands. "Is Sarah dead?"

Finn bangs his head on the table.

"Should I take them upstairs?" Sheralyn asks. Finn goes with her, but Olivia refuses.

"I suppose you'll have to know sometime." Dad sighs.

"That was Kate on the phone. The police have found a body. They haven't identified it yet, but we have to prepare ourselves. They think it might be Sarah."

I feel panicked. I was half expecting this, and yet I wasn't. I wasn't at all.

Olivia begins to cry.

"It might not be her," Mom tells us.

Dad hugs Olivia, who clings to him as she sobs in his arms.

I wish someone would hug me. Then Mom touches my shoulder and turns me to face her.

"Oh, Jemma," she says gently, and she squeezes my hand. I am so grateful, so relieved that she can sense my pain.

"Where...where did they find...the body?" she asks Dad.

"In Fox Woods," Dad says. "Kate's coming tomorrow to identify her. I'm relieved that they didn't ask us to do it." I see him shudder.

Olivia pulls away from Dad, her eyes red and face wet. Dad's shirt has a big wet patch too.

Mom goes and gives Olivia a squeeze, her eyes meeting Dad's. They know they can't promise us that it will be okay.

Later, when Olivia and Finn are in bed, I hear Dad talking to Mom. He says the police told Kate the circumstances "look suspicious."

They've found a body; Dan must have killed her. However much I try to think of a different explanation, I keep coming back to it. He killed Ryan, and now he's killed Sarah. And he taunted me with it. I can rage all I want. I can hate him more than anything, but it makes no difference. He knew he could do what he wanted.

I knew all along what he was like. And now it's too late.

32

When the doorbell rings after dinner, I'm sure it's him come to taunt me again, the keeper of his secret. Mom and Dad are upstairs, so Sheralyn goes out of the living room to answer it. I hear her say, "Can I help you?"

But it's not Dan; it's Richard.

He jabbers nervously. "Is Lorraine here? I... I'm Sarah's... I don't even know what to call myself—boyfriend, friend, ex-boyfriend—one of those... Who are you?"

Olivia sneaks out into the hall to see what's going on, just as Sheralyn explains that she is taking Sarah's place as my aide.

"I'll call Lorraine. She's upstairs," Sheralyn tells him. "Lorraine! Sarah's boyfriend is here," she calls loudly.

"He's not her boyfriend... Dan is!" Olivia blurts out. "He hasn't been her boyfriend for a while! Why are you pretending to be Sarah's boyfriend?"

"I'm not pretending. It's complicated," Richard explains. He sniffs.

"Anyway, Sarah's dead!" Olivia blurts out.

There's another loud sniff and Richard tries to speak, but Olivia interrupts him. "You're crying. Men don't cry."

"Olivia! Go back in the living room," Sheralyn tells her.

"Won't!" Olivia says with her usual stubborn tone.

"Please, Olivia—now!" says Sheralyn.

"I'm just telling the truth, so why should I be punished?" Olivia protests.

It's Mom to the rescue as she comes downstairs and invites Richard through to the kitchen.

"I'm sorry to drop in like this," he says. "The police came around. They've been asking more questions..." Richard's voice disappears into the kitchen. I strain to catch anything— try to tune out all other sounds—but it's no use.

My bag needs emptying. If Sheralyn takes me to the bathroom, there's a good chance I will hear something. I want her to notice, but she is still busy arguing with Olivia.

"I'm going upstairs," Olivia says finally. She seems to expect Sheralyn to protest, but Sheralyn says nothing and Olivia storms out and up the stairs.

I see Finn's clenched hand on the sofa relax as she leaves the room.

"I'll take Jemma to the bathroom, and then I'll be back," Sheralyn tells him.

As she pushes me in and turns me, I see that she hasn't fully closed the door. I strain my ears to hear.

"We don't know for sure that it's her," says Mom.

"They think I k—" says Richard. He swallows. "They think I've done something to her. They keep asking me—am I sure she got to the door, what did I do when I got home, can anyone confirm I was there?"

"No one saw you get home, then?" Mom asks.

"I live by myself," says Richard. "Nobody saw me go into my apartment." He's babbling now as his voice chokes up. "I love Sarah so much. I'd never hurt her. I'm not like that. I'd never hurt anyone."

"I'm sure you wouldn't," says Mom. I can hear Richard crying again.

"Anyway," says Mom, "we'll have to wait until the body's been identified. The police can't have any evidence against you or they'd have arrested you, wouldn't they?"

Sheralyn is taking longer than usual. She must be eaves-dropping too. Now that the conversation seems to be ending, she wheels me back quickly to the living room.

The police must be questioning Richard for a reason. Even though I want to believe him, Poirot says I should never rule anyone out.

33

The minutes crawl by the next day at school when all I can do is think about Sarah.

Kate phoned early this morning. She said she didn't think she could cope with identifying the body on her own. Mom was busy with us, so Dad said he'd go. I can totally understand her asking, but I do feel sorry for Dad. I know how he felt about it.

Sheralyn is at school and the rest of us are home now, waiting for them to come back, waiting to find out if it's her.

Olivia is not happy because she's had to miss ballet. I don't think Finn's aware enough to know he's missed his swimming lesson too. Mom has decided we should play Pairs to take our minds off things. I say *we*, but Mom and I are playing together, and Mom is mostly playing for Finn too. The cards are all laid out facedown in rows, and we take turns to pick two and see if they match. Mom is useless, which is frustrating because I have a good memory and could do much better than her if I could just pick the cards myself.

Finn is not very interested at first, but he suddenly begins to pick out matching pairs by himself. I've never seen him play a real game like this. Mom has to restrain him until it's his turn. He is beating Olivia, and I can see the tension building in her face. Finn has no interest in winning, of course. I don't think he knows what that means. He's just enjoying matching cards. Olivia will not cope well if she doesn't win, least of all if she is beaten by Finn.

Mom can see this too. She gives a brief lecture, supposedly to everyone, about winning not being everything and how not everyone can win.

Finn gets another pair. Then another. Olivia picks two cards. They match. *Phew!* She has another turn. This pair doesn't match. She throws those cards down and then kicks the rest of them so that they are all out of position.

"Olivia," Mom says sternly.

"I'm not playing this dumb game!" Olivia yells and storms out. I hear her feet thudding loudly as she thumps her way upstairs.

Mom sighs. She begins to put the cards in the box, but sees that Finn is still playing with them. He turns all the cards faceup and proceeds to match them into pairs and line them up. He is trying to make order out of the chaos.

The game had actually distracted me from thinking about Sarah, but now Mom's looking at her watch.

The doorbell rings. I see Mom jump.

Dad has his key—unless he forgot it. I wonder who it is.

I am facing the wrong way. I have to wait for a voice. "Hiya, any news?" a voice asks softly. Of course it's Sheralyn. I'm glad she's here.

As Sheralyn comes into the living room, I hear Mom's cell phone ring.

"Well?" says Mom.

It must be Dad. I wait, ears straining. "Oh, goodness," she says next.

Mom comes into the living room while Sheralyn is taking off her coat.

I see Mom's smile, but it is a small, sad smile. "It isn't her," she tells us. "The body isn't Sarah."

Mom flops down in the armchair, still clutching her phone to her ear, speaking into it. "See you soon, dear," she says.

I'm not sure if I'm crying or if my eye is just watering, but I can feel the wetness running down my cheek.

Finn stands up, looking almost as if he's going to say something. He turns and looks carefully at his lines of pairs. Every card is now matched, but one is slightly out of line. He straightens it and then claps his hands.

Has he heard what Mom said? I'm sure he has.

Sheralyn turns to Mom and then reaches out to give her a hug. Then Mom goes out into the hall, calling up the stairs for Olivia to come down.

"The body isn't Sarah," I hear Mom tell her.

"Where is she, then?" Olivia asks. "Where's Sarah? Why doesn't she come back?"

"If it turns out she's gone off somewhere on a whim," Kate says as we sit around the kitchen table with Mom and Dad later, "I will never forgive her for putting me through this—never."

That sounds weird to me. She has to be relieved that the body wasn't Sarah. But she and Dad just looked exhausted when they got back.

Kate starts to cry. "When they pulled back the sheet, I was so expecting it to be her, and then...and then..."

"It must have been awful," says Mom. She looks at Dad. I can't see his face, but his head nods slowly.

Mom goes over to Kate and puts a hand on her shoulder.

"That poor girl," says Dad. "The police don't know who she is."

Dad shudders. Mom goes over and gives him a hug. She kisses him, and he hugs her back. I can see the love between them, and it warms me inside, like the hot chocolate Mom's just made me that is the perfect temperature. People usually make it too cold because they're so worried about it being too hot!

Dad sits down and sips his coffee.

"Thank you for coming with me," Kate tells Dad. "It would have been much worse on my own. I just want to find her. I think she's alive and she's gone off somewhere to straighten her head out."

"I hope you're right," says Mom.

Soon after Kate leaves, I hear a sudden sobbing sound. It's Mom crying. I think she still blames herself for Sarah going missing.

Poor Mom. I wish I could comfort her and tell her it's not her fault.

And I need her to stay strong. If Mom goes to pieces, she might decide she can't look after us anymore. Then what would happen?

34

Mom's resting upstairs, and Dad and Sheralyn are looking after us. It's evening now, and Dan stands awkwardly in the hallway. Dad was wheeling me out of the living room when the doorbell rang, so I'm facing into the hall, wondering what Dan is doing here.

"I heard about the body they found," he says. "Thank God it wasn't her."

"Yes, Dan, it's a huge relief," Dad agrees.

"So there's no news at all—no more sightings or anything?" Dan asks.

There's something intense about the way he's asking this.

"No, nothing." Dad sighs.

I give an involuntary grunt, and Dad glances back toward me. "If only Jemma could speak," he says. "I often wonder what she'd be able to tell us."

"Yeah... I bet she knows all sorts of things," says Dan. He meets my eyes with a stare that makes me shudder.

Dad nods. "Lorraine took her to a specialist who thinks there might be a way for Jemma to communicate, but we've got to wait to be able to try it."

"Really?" There's a distinct edge to Dan's voice. His eyes flick over to me again. He watches me, and something clouds his expression. His lip twitches as if he is about to say something.

"Is there anything else?" Dad asks.

"No, no, I'll let you get back to what you were doing. I hope you don't mind me stopping by. It's just... I'm finding it tough, all this, you know."

"I'm sure you are. We all are," says Dad as he walks Dan out.

Dad comes back, sighing, and pushes me into the living room. I realize I must have been holding my breath because it all comes out in a rush. Dan's face when he found out about the specialist. He looked like he was suddenly seeing me differently. Like I might not be so powerless after all. He already wanted me out of the way. If he thinks I could tell his secret, what will he do?

The next morning there is something else for Mom to worry about—me. Maybe it's just exhaustion after everything with Jodi and the body and what Dad told Dan, but my back's aching again, and I worry it's another infection. I'm not sick enough to go to the hospital, thank goodness, but my temperature's up and I am too sick to go to school.

I think I'd rather be at school, to be honest, because I

don't want to be a strain on Mom, and at least at school there would be other things to think about. Here I can only think about Dan and Sarah and Jodi. I keep imagining Dan waiting outside the house. Figuring out when he could get me alone. I'm scared of Dan, and I'm scared I will never see Sarah or Jodi again.

I'm in bed. Mom checks me every ten minutes and takes my temperature. If it gets too high, I will have to go to the hospital. Every part of my body aches.

"I'm so sorry, Jemma." Mom sighs. "Life's the pits at the moment, isn't it?"

She's right. I feel so low—the lowest I can remember feeling. There's no point to anything anymore. I used to be content to watch, but now I don't like anything I'm seeing. Not being able to tell what I know is unbearable. I can do nothing, and Dan is running around free. I'm a complete waste of space. I'm a burden to everyone. I can't tell anyone about Dan. I couldn't protect Sarah. My own sister wanted to know me until she actually saw me, and then she changed her mind. What is the point of me being alive?

I feel so achy, so weak. They'll have to send me to the hospital soon.

Then I have a thought—a ludicrous thought. That would be Dan's chance, wouldn't it? That was how he got me on my own before. If Dan killed me and got caught, then they'd figure it all out.

I feel a weird elation, and my heartbeat races.

Maybe all these thoughts have finally made me crazy.

I'm getting hot and sticky. Mom takes my temperature again. She tuts. "It's too high, Jemma. This is no good. I'm going to call the hospital."

On this trip to the hospital I am aware of everything—every corner turned, every bump in the road. I don't want to live anymore. Not having a sister was okay. Having one but not seeing her is horrible. It was bad enough not being able to communicate, but having something I desperately need to say and not being able to say it is too much to take.

I am woken by a cough, a man's cough. It's not Dad. I'd recognize Dad's cough. I'm in the hospital—I can smell the disinfectant. There's a man standing close to me. Is it Dan? Has he come already? I can't see. I am facing the wrong way, but I can't see anyway. I try to focus, but my vision is blurry.

Right now I want Mom. *I want Mom!* A hand squeezes mine. It is a warm, soft hand.

"It's okay, Jemma. I'm here," Mom says gently.

"Ah, Jemma, you're awake" comes a man's voice from the other side of the bed. He has a strong accent. It's definitely not Dan.

"I'm Doctor Sargent," the voice continues. He speaks

slowly and loudly, as if I might not understand. Mom turns my head so that I can see a blurry white coat. The doctor is leaning over me. "You're doing poorly," he continues as if I don't know that, "and we've had to give you some medicine. Don't worry if your vision is a little fuzzy. It's a side effect, but it should settle down."

I am relieved to have an explanation for the blurriness.

Mom stays a long time, and I don't know how long she's been here already. I sleep and wake and sleep and wake, and she's still here. Now I wake and think she's gone, because I can't feel her hand, but I hear a snorting sound and then another. Mom's hand has slipped from mine, and she's actually asleep. She's snoring. Poor Mom. This is too much for her.

Dad comes eventually and takes over. Then Sheralyn for a while. They rotate. I mainly sleep. I dream about Dan.

"If I were you, I'd kill myself. Listen, if you ever want a little help, I could—"

In my dream I am able to nod, and then he is holding a pillow. It is coming down toward my face. I think, *This is it. This is the end.*

35

I've been here overnight. I know I will have to wait for Dan to find out I'm here, but I'm sure it won't take him long. Someone else comes—someone I'm not expecting.

It's Paula.

"This is so kind of you," Mom tells her. "I wouldn't leave Jemma with someone she doesn't know—but you know Paula well enough, don't you?" Mom looks at me and squeezes my hand. "It's just for a while. I have to go to Olivia's school."

I wonder briefly what's happened with Olivia. Has she hit someone else? Then my thoughts turn to Paula. My vision is clear again now, thank goodness. Paula's chunky-knit sweater does not disguise how thin she's getting. Her cheekbones are almost poking out of her face, and her hands look so bony there is barely any flesh on them. I hope she's not going to hold my hand. She shifts from one foot to the other anxiously.

It's taken courage to offer to do this, and I admire her for

I HAVE NO SECRETS

that, but I'm not sure I want her here. Actually, I'm sure I don't.

"It's no bother at all," Paula tells Mom. "You've been so kind to us. I'm glad to be able to do something for you."

"I've brought a book, if you feel like reading it to her," Mom tells Paula.

Paula nods.

Then Mom leaves.

Paula picks up the book and turns it over. I realize at once that she's not going to want to read it. It's not the vampire romance, though I'm not sure Paula would like that much either. It's a murder mystery! I hope she doesn't think Mom is too insensitive for suggesting it. Paula sighs and puts it down.

"Your mom says you understand everything, so I'm sure you do. I wish they'd catch Ryan's killer. I want to know what happened and why, and I want whoever did it locked up. Is that too much to ask, Jemma?"

She sounds like she's caught in a loop, like she's said the words so many times. I wish I could speak to her. I could change things.

"Between you and me, there's something I haven't told the police, Jemma, and I don't know what to do," she continues, leaning forward and speaking quietly. I had slightly lost concentration as she rambled on, but now I am alert.

"Before it happened," Paula tells me, "Ryan asked me to hide some stuff for him. I know I shouldn't have. I should've at least asked what was going on, but he clearly didn't want to tell me. I know I was stupid, but I did what he asked. I wanted to keep him out of trouble."

She pauses, and I want to ask, "What stuff?"

She edges even closer, and her voice is lower, almost a whisper. "It was jewelry, Jemma—diamond rings, gold necklaces—and I think Ryan might have stolen them," she says. "I didn't want the police to know he was a thief. They already knew he was a drug user. They might have written him off, not bothered to look for his killer. So I hid the things. I'm sure I shouldn't have, but I promised him and I hid them— and when the police came looking for clues, I didn't tell them. I couldn't cope with Graham finding out what I'd done, and I didn't want to get myself in trouble too."

I watch Paula. Her eyes look straight through me as if I'm not even here, and she's constantly rubbing her fingers together as she talks. It reminds me of Dan when Mom said the police were looking for him. It looks as if this guilt has been eating her up.

"It didn't occur to me at the time, but now I'm worried that the stuff belonged to the person who killed Ryan. What do you think, Jemma? I wish you could tell me. I bet you could figure it out better than me."

Maybe I *could* figure it out. I need to think...

"The thing is, I don't know what to do now," Paula continues, sighing. "Should I go to the police and tell them?

I'm scared I might get arrested for withholding evidence. I could say I just found them, but the police did such a thorough search, they might not believe me. How will Graham cope if I get thrown in prison? That's why I haven't even told him."

Paula suddenly sits up straighter. "I'm sorry, Jemma. I shouldn't be talking to you about this, should I? It's terrible of me. You're sick. You don't want to hear about Ryan— especially when you have Sarah to worry about too. Let's talk about something else."

But she clearly can't think of anything. She glances briefly at the book, but I can see she can't face picking it up. So we sit silently and she twiddles her thumbs.

I think about Ryan. I didn't know him well, but it sounds likely that he did steal the things Paula found. Why would someone kill him for that? Maybe he owed money for the drugs, and he stole the things intending to sell them. Could there be any link with Dan and Sarah? Maybe Ryan stole the jewelry from Dan, and that's why Dan killed him. Then Sarah found out, and he had to kill her too. The black jacket comes into my head. Could Graham have been involved? Could he have found the jewelry and confronted Ryan? Or could Graham have stolen it and Ryan found out? Then I remember Dan's face when Dad said I might be able to communicate.

Paula's phone beeps, and she pulls it from her bag in relief and continues to look at it, touching different areas of the screen for what feels like a long time.

36

Sheralyn takes over from Paula, and Mom comes back after lunch. I'm not feeling much better. I feel so, so tired.

Mom smiles as she sits down, and I notice she has big bags under her eyes. I want her here—but I also wish she could go home and get some sleep.

"I'm sorry I couldn't be here," she says. "I hope you were okay with Paula. Olivia's getting herself into all sorts of trouble at school." Mom is digging around in her bag as she speaks. "I've persuaded them to give her another chance, but I'm not sure she'll be able to stay there if she keeps starting fights. More parents have been complaining."

Mom's bag is bulging. An old shopping list, a pen, and a lipstick fly out, and she hastily retrieves them from the floor.

I hope Olivia isn't going to get herself thrown out of her school. I wonder what she did. I wish I could tell Mom what Olivia told me about Dylan.

"Here it is," Mom says finally.

It's a letter. I see right away that it is Jodi's writing on the front. My heart starts thudding, and my stomach churns. I don't know what to expect or how to feel. Jodi has written— but what has she said?

"I hope you don't mind that I opened it first," Mom says. "I didn't want to bring it if it was going to upset you. Not with you being so sick."

Mom pulls the letter out of the envelope.

Dear Jemma,

It's really hard to write this, but I hate thinking how upset you must be with me. I'll understand if you hate me and never want to see me again. I want you to know, though, that's not how I feel about you.

I want to explain what happened—or try to at least. I think I had a kind of image of you in my head, and I guess you didn't look anything like I was expecting. I know your mom sent a photo, but until I saw you, I had no idea how much you looked like me. I know we're twins, but I just wasn't expecting it for some reason. You must have seen that too. We are so alike!

You also—this sounds really bad, but I want to be honest—you look much more disabled than I expected. I knew you were in a wheelchair and that you can't speak, but it was a shock to see you.

I flinch as Mom reads this. She's referring to the strange shape of my head, my gaping mouth. I don't want to be a shock to look at, but there's not much I can do about that.

Mom continues.

I thought I'd just be able to start talking. I had so much I wanted to say that I wasn't worried about you not talking back. I'm quite a blabbermouth usually! No one else can get a word in. So I thought I would be okay.

I froze up, Jemma, and everything I wanted to say went out of my head. I felt so stupid standing there unable to speak. I don't know where the tears came from, but once I started, I couldn't stop, and I felt even worse so I had to just get out of there.

I want you to know that I do want to try again. You are my sister, and I want to know you and for you to know me.

Please, please forgive me, and let's start over— please!

Love, Jodi

My sister still wants to know me.

The warm feeling spreads through my body. I can even feel it in my legs and arms, and I can't feel much there usually.

"I can see that's brought some color back to your face!"

Mom exclaims. She strokes my cheek gently and touches my forehead. "Yes, it's not fever—just a healthy glow."

"When can I see her again?" I want to ask Mom.

She doesn't tell me, but I will forgive her for that because I am so happy about the letter. I wish I could hold it, smell it, keep it. I don't want Mom to fold it and put it in her bag. I wish she'd stick it on the wall beside my bed so I can look at it and read it over and over.

I try to remember the words as Mom puts her bag back on the floor.

You are my sister, and I want to know you.

That is all I need. I say it over and over in my head. From her to me, and me to her. I feel it. I live it. I don't want to die. I don't want Dan to kill me anymore, even if it would help the police catch him.

I feel the strength returning to my body all day.

I want to see Jodi. I need to get well.

37

Mom calls Jodi and arranges for us to meet her on Sunday. It's only two days to wait, but once I'm home, all I can think about is Sarah. Her absence is like a wide-open window through which a cold breeze constantly blows. I cannot feel warm and safe and happy, even knowing I will soon meet my sister again. What has happened to Sarah?

Mom still looks stressed out—and worse, she says Sheralyn has a bad cold and won't be able to help for a few days.

After dinner, Finn and Olivia go upstairs. Dad's not back yet because he has a late meeting at work. Mom pushes me out of the kitchen, saying she'll turn the TV on for me while she gets them ready for bed. As we reach the living room, the phone rings.

"Back in a minute," she tells me, sighing, and rushes off without even turning the light on, let alone the TV. I expect her to pick up the phone in the hallway and bring it back in here, but she must have taken it into the kitchen because her voice gets more distant.

She must be speaking quietly. I can't hear what she's saying or figure out who she's talking to. I hear the phone click, but it rings again almost immediately. I only hear "yes," "no," and "I should think so." Then "I'll let you know if I hear anything."

I can't believe Mom has left me here in the dark. I'm trying to hear her, but I get a sudden sense of someone behind me. I can hear breathing—loud breathing—as if someone is panting by the living-room door. My heart races. I'm not imagining it. Someone's here.

Has Dan gotten in? Was he waiting outside? He didn't come to the hospital, but he's here now! He's used Sarah's key to get in. He could have been in the house for hours—just waiting for the right moment.

The breathing is coming nearer.

"Mom!" I want to scream. "Get off the phone! Get in here now!"

He is right behind me. I feel my wheelchair jolt.

What is he going to do?

My chair jolts again. The breathing is still close, but... What's happened? The sound of breathing is right underneath me—under my chair!

There is a *bang, bang* against the right wheel. I suddenly realize it's Finn! Finn is under my chair, panting and banging his head against one of the wheels. I try to steady my breathing.

This whole Sarah thing must be affecting him badly. He's under my chair, wanting me to keep him safe, to make everything okay. He is trying to tell me how bad he feels. I wish I could do something—make everything better. I wish I could bring Sarah back.

At last I hear Mom's footsteps. But she doesn't come in. I hear her feet thump, thump up the stairs. She thinks Finn's up there. She's forgotten about me altogether.

She's gone up. Finn's breathing has slowed down, but I can still hear it. Mom's feet are soon on the stairs again because she hasn't found Finn.

"Finn! Finn, dear! Are you down here?"

She approaches the living room and turns the light on. She gasps.

"Jemma!" As she comes around in front of me, I am shocked to see she is sobbing. Tears are rolling down her cheeks. "I've left you here in the dark! I completely forgot! I'm so sorry. I'm so sorry, Jemma. I'm losing it. And I can't find Finn."

She collapses on the sofa, crying. I can't stand to see Mom like this. If Mom falls apart, Social Services will take us all away. It's a terrifying thought. She has to get it together. She can't let that happen!

At that moment, I hear Dad's key in the door.

He hears her sobbing and is by her side in seconds. "What's happened?" he asks softly. "Have they found her?"

"No, no—it's not Sarah, it's Jemma. I forgot her," Mom

sobs. "I left her in the dark when the phone rang. I left her in the dark for about twenty minutes! And I can't find Finn!"

Dad sees him right away. "That's easy, dear. Look, he's under Jemma's chair!"

"My God," Mom exclaims. "Finn, what are you doing there?"

Finn doesn't come out.

"If Sheralyn can't help, we've got to get the agency to send another aide," Dad says.

"Other families have to get by without aides," says Mom.

"Yes," says Dad, "but we wouldn't have taken on the other two if we didn't have help with Jemma."

"I didn't want to get someone else. Sarah... I thought she'd be back," says Mom, wiping her eyes with her sleeve.

"I'm sure she will," says Dad, though he doesn't sound convincing. "But in the meantime we need someone."

38

Dad has ordered Mom to take it easy, and the agency aide arrives after breakfast. She is smiley and bubbly, although her voice is a little loud.

"Hey, this must be Jemma!" she says.

"This is Rosie," Mom tells me.

"I can see we both like purple!" Rosie says, beaming at me. She points to my cardigan and her purple top. "We're going to get along just fine!"

Sarah chose that purple cardigan for me. I feel a pang.

Mom smiles at Rosie. "That's great. I'm so glad you could come so quickly," she says. "Let me tell you a little about Jemma."

"It's okay," says Rosie. "The agency filled me in. And I have lots of experience. You can leave us to get to know each other."

"Good," says Mom. "Just call me if there's anything you need."

There's an awkward silence as Mom heads off upstairs.

"I hear you like books," Rosie says. "I thought I could read to you, okay?"

I am relieved, although she's speaking strangely—not like she was with Mom.

She goes to her big purple backpack, which is on the sofa. "I always carry books with me!" she says. "Hang on a second—let me see what you might like."

I wish she'd just get the book that's on my nightstand, the one Mom's reading to me.

"Hey, this is a great one!" says Rosie. The singsong enthusiasm in her voice is already getting to me, but I will give her a chance. I look to see what book she's holding. The size of it and the brightly colored cover make me swallow hard. It's a fairy-tale picture book. *The Little Mermaid.*

This has to be a joke. No—she's wheeling me close to the sofa so she can sit beside me.

"I know you'll want to see the pictures!" she tells me, holding the book so it rests on my lap.

No one has told her I have a brain. She also hasn't thought to ask. I hope Mom will look in soon to see how she's doing and set her straight.

Mom doesn't come. I have to endure *The Little Mermaid* read in a patronizing voice with every picture pointed out. "Look, there's the mermaid!" "Look, there's a crab!" I don't even like the story of *The Little Mermaid*. Finally, it's over. "Do you like music?" Rosie asks me.

"I bet you do! I've brought some with me, specially." This sounds encouraging—though if it is Glowlight, I won't be able to stand it.

She pulls out her phone and swipes a few times. "Here we go!" I listen as the music begins. It's a baby song—"The Wheels on the Bus." This is utter humiliation. I am not a toddler in a teenage body; I am an actual teenager. I am sixteen!

She begins to wheel me around with dance-like movements, jerking me uncomfortably and singing along.

This is a nightmare.

Then I hear a laugh. It is a raucous, jeering kind of laugh. As I am spun around, I see Olivia standing in the doorway, laughing hysterically. The humiliation can't get any worse.

"Hey, do you want to join us?" Rosie asks her. "We're having a great time here!"

"You might be," says Olivia. "I don't think *she* is."

"No?" Rosie stops still. She turns me around to face her and looks at me closely. "It's hard to tell," she admits.

"She's not stupid," Olivia says.

"Of course not," says Rosie. "But she—"

"She's sixteen. She likes teenager stuff, not baby stuff."

"Thank you, Olivia!" I want to shout.

"Are you sure?" Rosie asks. "I thought bright colors and simple rhymes would be the right thing. I mean, how do you know what she likes or what she's thinking when she can't speak?"

"I just know," says Olivia. "I know lots of stuff, actually. I like teenage stuff too. I almost am a teenager."

"Really?" Rosie is looking more and more uncomfortable. "So how old are you?"

"Nine," Olivia says, "but I'll be a teenager in only four years. I know tons of things that teenagers know—tons."

"Okay," says Rosie. "So what do you suggest we do? What would you and Jemma—you teenagers—like to do now?"

Olivia looks thoughtful. I wonder what she's going to come up with.

"Watch TV?" she says. "We can watch *Fuzz Heads*. There's this really hot boy on it."

"Hot boy?" Rosie repeats, wide-eyed. "I'm not sure..."

"Mom lets me watch it. Even Finn watches it, and he's six," says Olivia.

"I'm not sure your mom will be happy to pay me to sit and watch TV," Rosie says doubtfully.

"I'm sure she will," says Olivia. "I promise you."

I don't like *Fuzz Heads*, but I am begging Rosie to agree.

"Okay—just for a few minutes," Rosie says.

"Yay!" says Olivia, plunking herself on the sofa.

When Mom comes down with Finn, I can see from her expression that she is not pleased we are watching TV.

"I read to Jemma and played her some music," Rosie assures Mom.

"Yeah—she put on nursery rhymes!" says Olivia.

"Nursery rhymes?" Mom exclaims. "Why would you do that?"

"I didn't know…" Rosie says. "I thought—"

"No, you didn't think!" Mom yells.

I am shocked to hear Mom raise her voice like this. It is so unlike her.

"You have to leave. Now," Mom tells her, pointing to the door. "Jemma is an intelligent young woman, and I cannot imagine how she felt. This is outrageous."

"I'm so, so sorry," Rosie says, her singsong voice gone and a feeble whisper coming out. "I really didn't mean—"

"Just go," says Mom.

Although I don't particularly like Rosie, I actually feel sorry for her in that moment—and surprised at Mom reacting so strongly. I'd have expected Mom to be upset and to explain, but I thought she'd give Rosie a second chance.

Once Rosie is gone, I see Mom grab a chocolate bar from between two books on the shelf and wolf it down.

After dinner, there's a call from Kate. Dad answers, and he looks shocked when he comes back into the kitchen.

"They arrested Richard yesterday," Dad tells us. "They've been questioning him, and they've applied for permission to hold him longer."

"*Richard?*" Mom says. "He seemed so nice and so genuinely upset when we told him she was missing."

"He was kind of a mess, if you ask me," said Dad. "I'm still surprised, though."

The police have the wrong man! I am sure of it. And while they're busy questioning Richard, they won't be thinking about Dan.

39

Last night I dreamed that Sarah came back—walked through the door as if nothing had happened. She said she'd lost her memory, and she had no idea where she'd been for the last few weeks. She put me to bed as usual and turned me in the night. She was smiling like she always did, and I knew that everything was going to go back to normal. Everything was going to be okay.

I woke this morning and had that sinking feeling I always get when I realize Sarah is still missing. I don't think everything is ever going to be normal again. Then I remember that today is not a normal day, not even a "normal without Sarah" day. Today I am meeting Jodi. I'm trying to wipe that first meeting out of my mind and just think about her last letter. The same thing can't happen again, I'm sure. This time we are meeting in a café. My social worker, Beth, and Donna, the social worker who came to support Jodi last time, are going to be there too.

The waiting was so awful last time that Mom has decided we should be a few minutes late in the hope that Jodi will already be there. Either that or we are just running late anyway!

Mom maneuvers my wheelchair into the café. It's big inside and not busy. I see Jodi with Donna and Beth, at a spacious table in the corner. She's here. My stomach wobbles. Donna sees us and jumps up to move chairs so I can get near the table.

"Hi, Jemma. Come and join us. Come and meet Jodi for real this time," she says.

Jodi gives me a quick smile and then turns away awkwardly. She looks stiff and terrified. I wonder if she is going to run off again.

Everyone says hello. Beth hugs me—I haven't seen her for a while. She looks from me to Jodi and smiles, talking in her low, soothing voice. "I feel quite emotional seeing you together. You can certainly tell that you're twins! I can imagine what a big deal this must be for both of you."

"I'm so glad you decided to come," Mom says to Jodi.

"It was hard." Jodi nods. "I was just...overwhelmed."

She looks quickly at me and back to Mom. "I hope she doesn't mind me saying that?"

I wish so much that I could smile at her, reassure her, tell her it's fine. It's enough that she's here.

"Don't worry so much," Donna tells her. "You'll be fine."

"I don't know what to say," Jodi continues, giving me

another brief, awkward glance. She fidgets anxiously on her chair. "Like last time, I could think of all sorts of stuff to talk about before I got here, but now here I am, and it feels so much harder..."

"You're getting yourself worked up," says Donna. "Don't upset yourself. Just start talking."

Jodi's face crumples. She looks even more like me for a moment. She's going to lose her nerve. I can see it in her eyes. She's going to get up and leave.

"Why don't you come closer and hold Jemma's hand?" Beth suggests. "I think Jemma would love that, and you don't need to talk at all unless you want to."

Jodi's shoulders seem to relax. She smiles gratefully at Beth, stands up, and moves her chair closer to mine.

She looks at me, her eyes still frightened, but there is warmth in them. I can see it. I can feel it.

"I'd like to hold your hand, Jemma," she tells me.

She touches, and then she squeezes gently. Her hand is soft and smooth and warm. It is the same size as mine, although mine is bony and clenched.

I feel a weird sense of connectedness. It is different from anyone else who has ever held my hand. This is my sister, my twin.

A waitress comes and takes our order for drinks. Jodi orders a smoothie, and Mom orders me an apple juice, asking for a straw.

Jodi says nothing, but I don't mind. Mom was right. I want her to talk at some point—I want to know all about her—but right now it is enough that my sister is holding my hand.

40

"What are your hobbies?" Beth prompts Jodi. "Maybe you could tell Jemma about them."

I'm so glad Beth's here. Donna is nice, but Beth's calmness and suggestions are definitely helping.

"Oh...well..." says Jodi. "I told Jemma some stuff already in my letters... I like reading." She starts off looking at Beth and then at Mom. "My favorite authors are John Green and Suzanne Collins. I've been reading *Paper Towns*. It's about a guy who goes on a road trip to find a girl. It's amazing."

"We read to Jemma a lot," Mom tells Jodi. "We'll have to look for that book."

"I can lend it to you," says Jodi.

"That would be wonderful," says Mom. "Maybe you could even read some to Jemma yourself?"

Jodi's face lights up. "Yes—I'd love to!"

I like the sound of the book. It's not the kind of thing I usually listen to, but I'd love Jodi to read it to me.

"I like sports too," Jodi continues. She's still talking mainly to Mom, but I can forgive her because at least she is talking now.

"I play field hockey at school. Maybe you could bring Jemma and come and watch one day."

I know nothing about field hockey, but watching Jodi play would be really cool. If I wasn't disabled, would I have been athletic too? It's not something I've ever thought about.

"That's great," says Mom. "I'm sure Jemma would love to."

The waitress comes at that moment with our drinks. "Do you want to give Jemma her drink?" Mom asks Jodi.

Jodi frowns. "No, I...I don't know. I don't want to spill it down her or something."

"Don't worry. Just watch me," Mom tells her. Jodi lets go of my hand, and Mom comes closer, pushing the straw carefully into my mouth.

"I could hold the glass now, if you like," says Jodi.

Mom passes it to her.

Jodi's face is close, very close to mine. I like that she's giving me my drink, the way she's focusing every ounce of her attention on me.

Mom slides her chair a little farther away and begins to chat to Beth and Donna.

"I'll tell you something else I like," Jodi says, putting my glass down carefully on the table. She clasps my hand in hers and continues. "Do you want to know my favorite band?"

For the first time, she is talking directly to me and not partly through Mom.

"I totally love Glowlight," she continues. "Have you heard of them?"

My heart almost stops beating. She loves Glowlight, just like me. And Sarah—poor Sarah. I wish I could speak. I wish I could tell Jodi all about the concert, about Sarah going missing.

"I wanted to go to their last concert a few weeks back, but I couldn't get tickets. I'd love to see them live one day."

She is still talking. Now that she's started, she can't stop. She's telling me about other bands she likes, some I've heard of and some I haven't—but I am thinking only of Glowlight. I can hear their lyrics in my head.

"Should I tell you more about me?" she says.

"Yes!" I want to say.

"So, I was adopted when I was eight months old, but I've always known. Maybe you've been wondering why my mom and dad didn't adopt you too," Jodi says anxiously.

"Don't worry, that's pretty obvious," I want to tell her.

"I think it's because we had different needs. That's right, isn't it, Donna?"

"Sorry—what?" Donna says. She's been talking with the others and not listening in, which pleases me.

Jodi repeats her question.

"Yes, Jemma. Jodi's parents never met you. You went to separate foster homes because your needs were very specialized. People who want to take in children who need special care like you need special skills—like your mom." She smiles at Mom. "You both have parents who love you. That's what matters, isn't it?"

I wish we had been able to stay together, though I realize what she's getting at. If we had, no one would have adopted both of us. At least on her own, Jodi had a good chance. And Mom and Dad are long-term foster parents, so it's not really different from being adopted. I couldn't ask for better parents than them.

"I think it's awful that we were split up," Jodi says to me. "My mom said the social worker told them they should tell me about you, but they decided not to. She said she realizes now they did the wrong thing. Anyway, I bet there's tons you want to ask me and tell me! I can't imagine how frustrating it must be not being able to speak. I think I'd lose my mind. I mean, I'm not saying you have, or that you're crazy or anything. You know that, don't you? I just mean it must be hard. I hope they get something figured out for you soon."

But she's right. I feel like I *am* going crazy inside—and she doesn't know half of what I need to say.

Mom stands up and comes nearer. "How's it going?" she asks.

"Great," says Jodi. "Thank you so much for giving me another chance." Jodi is reaching into her bag. She pulls out her phone. "Can you take a picture of us?"

"What a great idea!" says Mom. "I'm sure Jemma would like one too. I'll take one with my phone."

Jodi pulls her chair around beside mine, clutching my hand. Mom clicks away. I am delighted. I will have a photo of me and Jodi. I hope Mom will put it by my bed. I'm sure she will.

It's horrible saying goodbye to Jodi, and I want them to arrange another day to meet, but Jodi says we will and I believe her. And there is another nice surprise when I get home. Sheralyn's back. She's feeling better, thank goodness, and Mom is still looking so tired. Sheralyn isn't Sarah, but she's a great improvement over Rosie. Sheralyn reads to me. She has a nice reading voice, but she's not as good as Sarah. Sarah gave each character a different voice, and she read with such expression that I used to wonder if she'd ever tried acting.

I think she would have been good.

Mom printed the photo of Jodi and me, and now it is by my bed. I thought it might bother me that Jodi is beautiful and I am not, but when I look at the picture, all I see is the likeness. She is what I was meant to be—what I really am inside. Seeing her, I feel as if I am that beautiful. It makes me feel stronger. It's hard to explain, but I never imagined before that if I wasn't disabled, I might have looked so pretty. Now I can imagine it, and instead of feeling sad that I am not the same as her, I feel happy. I almost look as if I am smiling in the picture, and Jodi is definitely smiling.

Olivia comes to look at it.

"I wish I had a sister," she says.

I feel sorry for her. I want to say, "But I'm your sister, Olivia. We're a family—you, me, Finn, Mom, and Dad."

Olivia picks up the picture and holds it close to her eyes. I want her to put it back. I feel protective of it, and I'm scared she's going to scrunch it or even tear it.

Sheralyn comes in.

"Maybe I've got a sister too, like Jemma," Olivia says.

"Maybe," says Sheralyn. She sounds doubtful.

"Can you find out?" Olivia demands. "I want to know."

"I'll ask your mom," says Sheralyn, "but I think someone would have told you if you have a sister."

Olivia puts the photo on my nightstand, but she's laid it down flat so I can't see it. I panic. I feel an urgent need to see it, to keep it visible—as if Jodi might cease to exist or cease to be my sister if I can't see the picture of the two of us. I might wake and find it was all a dream. Sheralyn is my lifesaver. She notices and stands the picture up for me.

"Come on, Olivia—off to bed now," says Sheralyn.

41

I've been on a high since meeting Jodi. I enjoyed swimming at school yesterday, especially because the water was warmer than last week. Then in the changing rooms I overheard my teacher asking Sheralyn if there was any news about my aide, and I felt pangs of guilt. How can I even be happy for a second when Sarah is still missing? Last night I heard Dad tell Mom that Richard has been released, and I'm relieved about that, though Kate still thinks he did it. She thinks they just didn't have enough evidence to charge him. Everyone's so focused on Richard that they're missing the truth. They're not thinking about Dan.

Today, Sheralyn's gone to school. I'm ready for school, but my bus hasn't shown up. Mom phones and discovers it has broken down.

Finn's ride came, and luckily Dad was still here so he's taken Olivia. Mom says she'll take me to school herself.

She is pushing me out the front door when the phone rings

inside. She sighs, pulling me back a little and then pushing me forward. I can't see her face, of course, but I can tell she's not sure whether to take the call or not.

She pulls me jerkily back inside, and I hear her footsteps down the hall—running to pick up the phone. "Oh!" Mom sounds like she's walking toward the front door. There is real surprise in her voice, so much so that I actually wonder for an instant if it is Sarah herself calling.

"I wasn't expecting to hear from you. We got your letter, of course, but July... It's so far away..."

Professor Spalding! Why is he phoning?

"Really?" I hear Mom say. "Is he? When would that be?" There's a long pause. It seems to go on forever. Then finally she says, "Yes, I'm sure that would be fine." And there's silence again, but I can hear that she's taking notes.

A few minutes later, Mom is back, pushing me out the door again.

"Well, it's good I took that call, Jemma," she says. "The researcher from Israel who has created the sniffing technology decided at short notice to come to a conference here this week, and Professor Spalding says he wants to meet you."

What? I can't believe this. He's actually here?

"Mr. Katz would like to try his sniffing equipment with you. He wants us to meet him tomorrow!"

The waiting room at the University Hospital for Neurology and Neurosurgery is big and busy. Hospitals to me always mean long waits. Mom gets a coffee from the machine, so she is clearly thinking the same.

"I don't want you to get your hopes up too high, Jemma," Mom says quietly. "If this doesn't work, don't worry. We'll keep trying until we find a way. Technology is developing and changing so fast."

From a look at her face, I can see the hope in her eyes. I heard the high-pitched excitement in her voice after she hung up the phone yesterday. She does believe it; I'm sure she does. But do I? What if I can't do it, or I can't master it quickly enough and they decide it won't work? Will they give me a chance to practice?

Nurses with lists have been calling people, but then I see a man in a suit with dark hair, tanned skin, and a beard come into the waiting room and look around.

He spots me. I see his eyes stop and his bushy eyebrows go up. He walks confidently toward us.

"Jemma Shaw?" he asks, looking at me and then Mom. He has a strong accent and a serious expression. I wish he'd smile. Maybe he doesn't think this will work either.

Mom stands up quickly and introduces us.

"Alon Katz," the man says, nodding at each of us and then holding his hand out to Mom. "Please follow me," he tells us.

He heads off through the double doors and along a corridor, into a small room.

"I am sorry it is a little tight for space in here," he says as Mom awkwardly parks me between a chair and a desk.

She sits down on the chair beside me and squeezes my hand as Mr. Katz picks up glasses from the desk and puts them on. In front of him is what looks like a thin plastic tube with some pieces sticking out of it.

"This is it," he tells us. "This is the sniff controller. It is still in the research phase, you understand. We have had success using this equipment with patients suffering paralysis following accidents, even with some who were thought to be in a vegetative state. We have not tried it on someone with cerebral palsy, and my colleague Professor Spalding thought you would be an interesting case for me."

I can't see Mom's face, but I wonder if she is as surprised as I am. I expected some complicated machine or something—not just a plastic tube.

"We attach this with these sensors just inside the nostril," he explains. "The other end can be attached to whatever a person is trying to control—a computer, a communication device, even the movement of a wheelchair."

"Really?" says Mom. "It looks so...simple."

I see what I am sure is a slight smile behind the beard of Mr. Katz.

"First, I will check your ability to control your sniffs,"

he says, approaching me. He has the tube in his hand. "This won't hurt," he tells me, "but it may feel a little odd at first, having something in your nose. The sensor is tiny, though."

He leans very close into my face. I can feel his breath, hot against my cheeks. One hand is on my chin, holding my head steady. I wish my head would stop pulling away from him. He might think I'm objecting, but it's just my body not behaving. I want to try this. I really do.

He stands back. My nose does feel strange—a little tickly. I hope I don't sneeze the thing out.

"We will attach it to this computer," says Mr. Katz, fiddling with the other end of the tube. "Now, you see this on the screen? This line here will move when you sniff. Try a small sniff, Jemma—in through your nose."

Oh, marvelous. I feel so nervous I think I've forgotten how to sniff!

"In through your nose," he repeats gently.

I must. I can do it. He must see I can do it. I sniff. The green line bounces on the screen. *I did it!* I made that happen. I do it again, even though he hasn't told me to. I want to see the line move.

"Good...good," he says slowly. "Now try a bigger sniff."

I do it—and right away the line soars up the screen.

"There." He grins, and I think this is the moment he is sure. The little sniffs might have been accidental, but this time he knows it is for real.

"Another big one, please," he asks. The line soars again.

"Now a small one."

This is easy. I can do this—I really can. I can make things happen!

I practice this a little more, and then Mr. Katz presses a few keys on the keyboard. The screen with the line disappears. I feel disappointed. I could have kept doing that all day. I was making the line move. I was doing it myself. I don't want to stop now.

There is something else on the screen.

"On this screen you will see two words," he tells me. "YES on one side on the green background and NO on the other side on the red."

He points to the words. I want to say, "I can read. I don't need you to point," but I try to stay calm.

"You will see the cursor here is constantly moving from one word to the other, every few seconds? I will ask you a question. You will sniff when the cursor is on the answer you wish to give. Okay? Big sniff when the cursor is where you want it."

This is my chance to communicate. *This is it!* What is he going to ask me?

"Do I have a beard?"

What?

It takes me a moment to take his question in. He is very still. So is Mom. I can hear them both breathing. I must stay calm. I can do this. I already know I can.

I wait for the cursor to move. I do a big sniff.

"YES," says a loud woman's voice.

I lurch inside. I didn't expect the computer to actually speak the word. The YES on the green side of screen is flashing too. But it is the voice that I can't get over.

"Good. Let's try another one. Is the wall in this room red?"

The cursor is on NO. I am worried it will move to YES before I manage to sniff. I sniff quickly.

"NO," says the voice.

I am ready for it this time, but I am still enthralled to hear it.

I have a voice.

42

Mr. Katz asks a few more questions—pointless questions like "Is the sky blue?" and "Do dogs have six legs?" Then he asks, "Do you like the sniff controller?"

I do a big sniff for "YES." Then two more. "YES. YES." Mr. Katz smiles a big smile.

He turns to Mom. "Would you like to ask Jemma something?"

"Gosh," says Mom, coming around to face me. "There are so many things I want to ask. I can't think..."

Mom hesitates.

"Meeting Jodi..." she says finally. "Are you glad you met her? Please be honest, Jemma."

"YES," I sniff.

Mom stares at me, her eyes open wide as she takes in the fact that she's asked me a question, and I have answered it. I can't quite believe it either.

Her lip quivers, and she rubs her eye. Her mouth opens and

then shuts again. Then she smiles. "Good. I'm so relieved," she says. "I hoped so much that it was the right thing."

"YES," I sniff.

I wish the voice of my *yes* had as much enthusiasm as I feel. I sniff "YES" and "YES" again just to be clear.

"Now let's try a letter board," says Mr. Katz. "I understand from Professor Spalding that you can read, Jemma, but don't worry too much about correct spellings."

Things are moving fast. Am I ready for a letter board?

I watch as a screen with three panels appears. One is the alphabet spread across four rows. The next is numbers. The third panel is an empty green block. Underneath these three is a wide white block. YES and NO was one thing, but how can I possibly control this?

"This is very basic software that you can use to spell out words," Mr. Katz explains. "The sniff controller can be linked to any communication software on a computer or tablet, so if this works, a speech therapist can help to identify the best software for you."

Mr. Katz points at the screen. "As with the YES and NO screen, the cursor moves between the blocks, as you see. If you want a letter, give a big sniff when you reach the letter block. The cursor will then move from row to row. Give a small sniff when it reaches the row you want. The cursor will then move along that row, and you can select a letter with another small sniff. What you type will appear in the white box below. In the green box you will see predictive text, but don't concern yourself with that for now."

I am starting to feel panicky. This is meant to be basic? I'm not going to be able to do it. It's too hard—I can't take it all in. And what if I spell the words wrong? "Let's try a letter," he suggests. "See if you can select the letter *C*."

I try to remember how to do it. I am relieved when he reminds me.

I wait as the cursor moves between the screens.

I sniff. It isn't that different from picking yes or no. "Choose the row with a small sniff."

C is in the first row. The cursor goes past before I can sniff, so I wait for it to go through the rows and back to the first. This time I do it!

"Now another small sniff when you reach *C*," says Mr. Katz.

I've done it! *C* has appeared in the white box.

After a few minutes, with Mr. Katz's patient instructions, the word *CAT* is visible at the bottom of the screen. It is slow, but I am writing words, real words, for the first time in my life.

"Do you want to type something yourself?" he asks me. "Maybe tell us how you feel about the sniff controller."

I panic now. What do I say? What are the best words to express how incredible this is? Amazing? Brilliant? These feel right, but they will take forever. Good? Great? Slowly I begin to sniff out the word *GREAT*. I type *G R*, but sniff too late for the next *E* and get *F*. I've typed *GRF*. What do I do now? How do I correct a mistake?

Mr. Katz sees I have stopped sniffing. "If you make an error, select this eraser symbol to get rid of the last letter," he tells me. "And this"—he points—"is the space bar, if you need it."

Yes, now I can do it! I erase the *F* and sniff the *E* instead. Then *A*, then *T*.

"If you select the red speaker button—bottom right, here—then it will speak your words," says Mr. Katz.

It takes a few sniffs to get there, but then it happens. The voice says, "GREAT."

"You are doing so well," says Mr. Katz. "I think *you* are great, Jemma!"

"So do I!" says Mom. Then I hear sniffing—and it's not me. There is a sob. Mom is crying.

I begin to type *DONT CRY*. It takes about five minutes for me to get the right letters. Mom watches. I select the speaker. Mom cries harder.

"Sorry, Jemma," she says between sobs.

"Let me fetch you a glass of water," says Mr. Katz, handing Mom a tissue.

He leaves the room, and only now do I wonder what happens next. When can I have one? It might take a while to order it, I guess. Will it have to come from Israel? I need to type something now while I have the chance.

I am about to sniff toward the *D* when Mr. Katz comes back in with a glass of water and gives it to Mom.

"You have worked very hard and must be tired," he tells me. "It is best not to do too much the first time." He presses something on the computer, and the screen disappears. He pulls the tiny sensor tubes from my nostrils.

"No!" I want to scream. I find myself sniffing as if to select *NO* through my nose, but of course I am disconnected now.

"I know you have waited a long time for this moment, Jemma," says Mr. Katz.

"All her life," says Mom.

"And I am sure you are impatient to have the system at home."

Yes, I am! He's switched it off now, but maybe he'll let me take it home with me.

"I'll have to ask you... How much does it cost?" Mom says.

I freeze. What if it is too expensive? What if I can't have it at all?

Mr. Katz smiles. "You will be surprised," he tells Mom. "This is unusually cheap to make. As you can see it's low-tech. It's really just a plastic tube. It doesn't rely on advanced technology of the kind used for eye-gaze sensors or vocal cord hummers, although it can be connected to many devices running all kinds of software."

So it's not too expensive! When can I have it? "However,

it is still, as I say, in the research phase and has not gone into production yet," Mr. Katz continues. "This equipment is just a prototype."

My heart sinks. How long will I have to wait?

Can't I just have this one?

"So how soon would Jemma be able to have one at home?" Mom is asking exactly what I want to ask. I can see the disappointment on her face too.

Mr. Katz's feet shift as he wrinkles his forehead. "I have seen, Jemma, that you can use the equipment successfully. I will speak to my team and find out if I can leave this one with you. If so, I would require you to report on your use of it as a participant in our research project. We're leaving in two weeks, but someone on the team can bring it over to you and set it up before we go."

The significance of this slowly sinks in. I had an opportunity to say something here and now, and I've missed it. I've got so much that's so important to say. Instead of typing *CAT*, I should have typed *DAN KILLED RYAN*.

43

Mom and I have lunch in the hospital cafeteria. She leaves me by a table where I can see her and goes to get the food. I watch her pull out her purse to pay, and she has a puzzled expression. She searches her bag.

"I must be going mad," she tells me, plunking down a tray. "I'm sure I had twenty dollars in my purse. Lucky they take credit cards."

I think about Olivia. Has she been taking money again?

Mom sits down next to me. "That sniff controller's amazing, isn't it?" she says as she spoons soup into my mouth. I am conscious of people watching, but I don't care. I wish I could tell them—all of them. *I can communicate now. I can talk!*

Mom phones Dad and tells him all about it. She sounds so excited. Then she listens while Dad speaks. I wish I could hear what he's saying.

He greets me warmly when we get home. "Such wonderful news, Jemma. You'll be bossing us around and telling us what's what soon!"

I wish!

"All okay here?" Mom asks as she pushes me into the kitchen. Dad follows.

"Yes. Dan phoned," Dad tells her.

"Oh?" says Mom.

Dan—what did he want?

"Yes, he just wanted to know if we'd had any news about Sarah," says Dad. "He's very worried, like we all are."

"It must be hard for him all alone," says Mom. "At least we have each other for support."

I cringe inside as she says this. The only thing he's very worried about is getting caught.

"Yes, I think he sees himself as a family guy. He said he was eager to settle down with Sarah, start a family with her," says Dad. "He asked how the kids are doing, and I told him the good news about Jemma. He sends his congratulations. He was very interested in how it works. He said to tell you, Jemma, that he'd love to come and have a talk with you sometime."

"It's nice to have something positive happening," says Mom, sighing.

Panic surges through me as I take in what Dad said. He has told Dan that I can communicate! Dan is never going to let me tell his secret. No wonder he's very *interested*. His message to me was a threat, I know it. I feel like I was at the top of a hill, happily looking at the wonderful view, but someone has left the brake off my wheelchair and now I'm rolling down, down, faster and faster, heading straight toward a busy street. It doesn't sound like Dad told him I might have to wait two weeks. Dan won't take the risk. He won't wait. He'll have to kill me now, won't he?

I'm scared. I will for someone to stay with me at all times, but later I find myself alone in the living room watching TV. Finn and Olivia are upstairs. Mom is cleaning the table from dinner. I'm not sure where Dad is.

I don't feel safe on my own. I can't stop thinking about Dan. I am alert to every little sound, though it's not as if I can do anything. I thought this sniff controller was going to change my life. I thought I had a future ahead of me, that I was going to have the chance to get to know my sister. I was stupid. The sniff controller is amazing, but Dan can't let me use it, can he?

If only I'd told Mom about Dan while I was trying it. Then someone could have done something, and I wouldn't be so frightened now. I missed my chance. I know he's going to come. I can feel it.

I try to watch the game show on TV. I force myself to concentrate, but I don't know any of the answers. Ten, maybe fifteen minutes pass. Maybe he won't come yet. Maybe he'll wait until I'm in bed.

Then I hear a car pull up somewhere outside, a car door

slam. Is that him? Could it be? I wait, look at the TV. He'll
have Sarah's key—he could slip in, so quietly. A minute or
two passes. There is a sound behind me. The living-room door
clicks shut. That door should be open. I hear another sound.
Someone took a breath. I can't see toward the door, only
the TV, but I know. Someone is here, in this room, standing
behind my wheelchair.

My heart beats faster. I find myself sniffing, picturing the
letter board and spelling *HELP* as if a miraculous imaginary
sniff controller might respond by blurting out, "HELP! HELP!"

Nothing's happening, but I can definitely hear breathing—
very close behind me. What is he waiting for? *Come around in
front of me. Let me see you.*

He's moving—as if he's heard me. *I want Mom!*

I want Mom! I am as helpless as a baby.

A knife glints in my face.

44

The knife—a small, sharp blade—is so close to my face that it is blocking my view of anything else. I've not seen a knife like this except on TV. I think you'd call it a switchblade.

As my eyes focus, I see that the shape of the person behind it is small. The knife is held in a small purple-gloved hand. These can't be Dan's hands or gloves. The knife moves back a little. It isn't Dan.

"I know you saw," Olivia says quietly. "I know you saw, and I know you'll tell on me."

Olivia. Where did she get the knife? Why is she waving it at me?

"I know you saw," she says again.

I have no idea what she's talking about.

The knife is in front of my eyes. It wavers in her shaking hands. I wish she'd drop it. It's so close. It's almost scratching my cheek. I can't control my head movements. If my head jolts the wrong way, that knife will slice me.

My head jerks suddenly, as if it's heard my thoughts. I tipped away from the knife and not toward it, but I know that was pure luck.

"I've got to make sure you can't go telling on me." There is venom in her voice though she speaks barely above a whisper. The knife is steadier. "If you tell anyone I stole Lorraine's money, they'll throw me out of here." She's breathing hard. I'm in shock. It's about the money she took from Mom's purse. She didn't think I'd ever be able to tell anyone. But now she knows I will.

"I like you, Jemma," Olivia continues, "even though you don't do anything." She screws up her face. "But I can't let you tell. I'll do it quickly, okay? No one will think it was me."

She pulls the knife slowly back, ready. She can't be serious. But I can see the determination in her pressed-together lips. She means it. She's going to do it. *Mom! Mom! I need you!*

"*Olivia!*"

Suddenly Dad is there. "What the—? For God's sake, Olivia. Where did you get that knife?"

Olivia jumps, and the knife jolts wildly in front of my face. I think I feel it scrape my cheek.

"Give it to me," says Dad.

Olivia is shaking, harder and harder, but she doesn't let go of the knife.

"Olivia. Give it to me now," Dad says again. His voice is low, calm, and serious.

She drops the knife. Dad quickly grabs it and shuts it. Olivia is sobbing now, wailing. She curls up on the floor and rocks like Finn.

Saliva gathers in my mouth. I can't swallow. Would she have done it? Could she really have stabbed me? I don't know. It's hard to believe she would.

Dad's face is white with shock. He stands, paralyzed for a moment, staring down at Olivia on the floor.

"Lorraine!" he yells loudly. "Can you come in here?"

Mom runs in. "What's happened?" Her voice is high, panicky.

"I found Olivia holding this knife out as if she were about to stab Jemma."

Dad flicks the knife open and shut again for Mom to see.

"*What?*" Mom exclaims. She comes around in front of me, looking at me anxiously and then at Olivia.

"Olivia! Calm down. What on earth were you thinking?"

Olivia is still sobbing loudly and doesn't look like she's about to calm down.

"We need that sniff controller," says Mom. "We need Jemma to be able to tell us what's going on."

And she has no idea how much I need to say!

Mom sits on the floor and puts a hand on Olivia's shoulder. Olivia pushes her away. Dad is holding the knife, staring at it with a bewildered expression.

"That's not ours, is it?" Mom asks him.

"No," Dad says firmly.

"Just tell us one thing, Olivia," says Mom. "Where did you get this knife?"

Olivia sobs for what feels like minutes before she finally says, "I...f-found...it. I f-found it in the y-y-yard."

"In *our* yard?" Dad says. "Where exactly?"

"My ball...went into the bushes right at the back, and... and...something was sticking up in the mud behind the shed, and I p-pulled it."

"When was this? Why didn't you tell us?" Dad asks.

"Weeks ago. I...I wanted to keep it," says Olivia. "Just in case."

"In case of what?" Dad demands. Olivia shrugs, but says nothing.

"Why *Jemma*?" Mom steadies her voice. "Why were you pointing it at *her*?"

Olivia's shoulders are shaking. She begins to sob again.

"Come upstairs with me," Mom says firmly.

I wonder if Olivia will tell her the truth.

As Mom leaves, I hear Sheralyn coming down. "Is everything okay?" she asks. "I heard shouting..."

Dad goes out into the hall, and I can hear him telling her what's happened.

"That is one messed-up kid!" says Sheralyn.

"I know," says Dad. "I don't think we realized how bad it was. I'm not sure what'll happen now."

I wonder what he means, what will happen to Olivia. It's only when I am lying in bed later, unable to sleep, that I think about the knife. How did a knife end up buried in our garden?

Could it possibly have been the knife Dan used to kill Ryan? Dan goes into the garden to smoke sometimes. Olivia might just have found the most important piece of evidence, and she has no idea.

———————

Olivia is staying in her room, and Mom has taken some breakfast up to her. She says Olivia won't get out of bed and won't talk.

Finn is eating his cereal slowly and deliberately. He seems to be checking carefully that each wheat square has four sides before it reaches his mouth.

Dad doesn't go to work.

"I'm going to call Mr. Katz and find out when the sniff controller is coming," he tells me as he feeds me breakfast.

It's hard to swallow. I feel stuffed so full of things I need to say that there is no room for food.

I'd like to hear the call, but once I've finished eating and been wiped up, Dad goes into the living room with the phone.

He comes back looking pleased. "Thank goodness. They say it's coming tomorrow," he tells me. "Someone named Mr. Fogel is bringing it."

Tomorrow.

When Mom comes down, Dad tells her about Mr. Fogel. And he says that Olivia's social worker will be over in half an hour.

Mom decides I should go to school, that it is best to keep things normal. I think they want me out of the way while they deal with Olivia.

When I get home, Olivia has gone. Mom explains that her social worker has found her somewhere else to stay for a while.

"I don't know if we'll be able to have her back here. She won't say what happened," Mom says, shaking her head and sighing despairingly. "I still can't believe it. I'm so sorry, Jemma. It must have been terrifying."

Finn is home. He isn't playing or lining things up either. He just sits rocking. I hope he is okay. I hope Olivia will be okay too.

45

The next morning, the hour and a half between Finn leaving for school and the time the sniff controller is due to arrive passes so slowly I wonder if the clock on the living-room wall has stopped. I'm starting to get a headache.

At last there is a ring at the door. He's here!

Mr. Fogel introduces himself and tells me it's great to meet me. He says it with such enthusiasm it's like I'm a celebrity or something. He says I'll be set up in no time.

"No time" turns out to be another hour. First he has to download the communication software onto Mom's tablet. From the frown on his face, I think he's having problems. What if he can't get it working? I hope I'll be able to sniff okay—be able to work it. What if the other day was a fluke, and this time I can't do it at all? I try to practice while I wait. My headache gets worse.

"When you have a moment, I've got some forms I need you to sign to say you're happy for Jemma to be part of our research project," says Mr. Fogel. "And then we'll go through the records we need you to keep." He switches his gaze to me. "I wanted to try this out with someone with a disability like yours, and it's great to have the opportunity."

I wish he'd get on with it. He has no idea about the urgency.

"Here we go. Sorry it's taken so long," he says finally.

He puts the sensors into my nostrils and turns the screen so that I can see it.

"Now, I know you've worked with this—but haven't had much chance to practice yet! We'll start with the YES and NO screen. Big sniff when the cursor is on your choice of word. Are you ready?"

I am flummoxed for a moment. I wish my head would stop thumping. How do I tell him I'm ready? Then I realize. A big sniff!

"YES," speaks the voice.

"Great! Good job. Can you see the screen clearly enough?"

"YES," I sniff.

Then we switch to the letter board. He gets me to spell a few words, which I do, slowly and carefully. I guess it may seem slow for someone listening, but I can do it! The thrill of it surges through me all over again. It's like a kind of magic.

"Would you mind if I asked Jemma some things in private?" Mom asks.

"Of course," says Mr. Fogel. He smiles at me as he heads off toward the kitchen.

"Jemma," Mom says softly. "Do you know why Olivia was threatening you?"

The seriousness of what I have to say brings me back down to earth.

"YES," I sniff.

"Please tell me," says Mom.

I hesitate. I want to answer Mom, but I am not sure she is asking the most important question. I need to talk about Dan—and Sarah. Is it wrong to answer the question I want to answer rather than what Mom is asking? Will it confuse her? I feel panicky. I'm not used to having to make decisions like this!

I begin to spell. I select *D*. But when I try *A*, I miss and get *B* so I've typed *DB*. How do I erase a letter? I panic. Then I remember there is an eraser key.

I select it. Now I'm back to *D*. I wish I could do this faster. At last I have sniffed *DAN*.

"Dan?" Mom repeats, clearly confused.

I ignore her. I have to think how to do a space... Yes, I've selected a space. I need to explain, but I want the fewest words. I spell *RYAN*, hoping she will get what I mean. Sometimes I pass the letter I need and have to wait for the cursor to go around again. I know Mom is watching. I don't know what she's thinking. I have to concentrate. I select the microphone, and the voice says, "*DAN RYAN*"—although I know Mom has already read what I've typed. Hearing it aloud, I feel suddenly overwhelmed. My head spins.

220   PENNY JOELSON

"Dan Ryan?" Mom repeats. Her eyes are wide. "Is this to do with Olivia?"

"NO," I sniff.

"You're telling me something else. Am I right?" Mom asks.

"YES," I select, with relief.

Mom pulls her chair close to me. "Jemma, what are you trying to tell me about Dan and Ryan?"

"KILL," I slowly sniff.

"What? Dan killed Ryan?" Mom asks. "Is that what you're saying?"

"YES," I sniff.

"How do you know this?"

"TOLD ME," I sniff.

"Who told you?"

"DAN," I sniff again. Then I keep sniffing because I don't want another question. Mom waits patiently.

"KILL SARAH TOO."

Mom's eyes are even wider. "Jemma, wait. I need to call the police. I don't want to make you tired—I know it's a lot of effort. We'll speak to the police together."

Mom phones the local police station and explains. When she says, "Jemma has important information," I feel relieved. I just hope I can explain clearly and that they'll believe me.

"They'll be here in half an hour," Mom tells me. "Do you want to rest?"

I am aware that I haven't answered Mom's question about

Olivia. Although I'm tired and my head is spinning, that feels important too.

"OLIVIA," I sniff.

"You want to tell me about Olivia?" Mom gives me an encouraging smile. "I'm all ears, Jemma."

"MONEY," I sniff.

"Money?" Mom frowns. "PURSE," I sniff.

Mom hasn't gotten it yet. She's frowning as she tries to piece it together. I'm not being clear enough—this is so hard!

"Olivia took money from my purse?" Mom says at last.

"YES," I sniff.

"I thought money was disappearing. I had no idea it was her. But why was she threatening you with a knife?"

"I SAW," I sniff.

"She thought you would tell me?" Mom asks. "She was scared?"

"SENT AWAY," I sniff.

"She was scared she'd be sent away? What a mess!" says Mom. "But we can't keep her here after what happened."

"SAD," I sniff.

"Yes, Jemma, I'm sad too. Do you know why she took the money?"

"NO," I sniff.

Mom suddenly holds her head in her hands. She has tears in her eyes.

I feel bad. I didn't want to make Mom cry. "Social Services weren't sure about placing her here, but I convinced them. I thought we could help her." It is Mom sniffing now. "Maybe this wasn't the right place. And everything with Sarah means we've been giving her a lot less attention than she needs. What useless foster parents we are. We're supposed to be keeping you all safe!"

No! I don't want Mom to feel useless and sad! "YOU GOOD," I spell. "LOVE YOU."

"Thank you, Jemma. I love you too—so much. I'm going to phone Ben. I think he needs to be here. I still can't take all this in."

I'm thinking about Olivia, about how terrified she was of being sent away—so terrified that she pointed a knife at me. And now her worst fears might come true. I'm sure she didn't mean to hurt me. I'm sure she wouldn't do it again. When she first came, Olivia never really felt like part of our family, but now she does. Since she's confided in me about things, I've started to feel like a big sister to her, and now that I'd be able to talk to her, I could be that even more.

"OLIVIA STAY," I tell Mom.

"What? I'm not sure, Jemma. Not after what she did..."

"STAY," I repeat. "FAMILY."

Mom sighs and wipes her forehead. She looks like she has a headache, and I think her hands are shaking.

My own headache is getting worse. I wish someone would

give me some painkillers. We wait. Then I suddenly realize I can actually ask for some!

"HEAD PAIN," I sniff.

"Of course. I'll get you some painkillers," says Mom. I am stunned at how easy this is. *I can communicate!*

I really can! And I don't have to stay in pain with no one knowing. This is huge!

46

While we wait for the police and for Dad, I have a break from sniffing. It takes a lot of effort. The painkillers start working. My headache is still there, but easing off.

Mr. Fogel seems unsure what to do once Mom has explained what's going on. He tells Mom he feels he should stay a while longer in case anything goes wrong with the sniff controller, but he doesn't want to be in the way. Mom reassures him and makes him a cup of coffee. He comes to sit with me in the living room and tells me more about his research, how he is a neurobiologist specializing in olfaction—which he says is all things to do with the nose and sense of smell. They came across the idea of sniffing as a means to control things purely by chance. I am fascinated.

"I never imagined one day I'd be sitting with someone who is using the sniff controller to give a crucial witness statement to the police!" he says, giving me a big smile.

Then Mom turns on the TV, and Mr. Fogel and I watch a program about people who want to move to Australia.

Mom phones Olivia's social worker to tell her what I said. She's in the kitchen, but I can hear snippets. It sounds like Olivia can't come back. I feel sad.

Dad's home. Mom starts crying when she tells him about Olivia. He hugs her, and then he comes and hugs me too, so tightly I worry he might pull out the sensors in my nose.

"I think I'm still in shock," Dad says.

The police arrive. They're the same two that came when Sarah first went missing. Dad takes his newspaper into the kitchen for Mr. Fogel to read while he waits. So I have Mom, Dad, Officer Hunt, and Officer Sahin in the living room with me. Mom explains to the police how the sniff controller works and that I have just gotten it and haven't had much practice.

"Can you tell us what you told your mom?" Officer Sahin asks.

It is very slow, but now I see how I can use the predictive text, which makes it slightly quicker. Even so, by the time I've spelled a word, Officer Hunt is already fidgeting impatiently.

"DAN KILL RYAN," I sniff.

Officer Sahin has been watching the screen, but she looks startled as the voice finally speaks my words.

"And you know this because?" she asks.

"TOLD ME," I spell again.

"Who told you?" she asks.

"DAN," I sniff. "WONT CATCH ME."

"Dan won't catch you?" Officer Sahin asks.

I thought I was doing well—I'm definitely getting faster—but I'm frustrated now. "NO," I sniff. I try to think how to be clearer.

"Ahh—are you telling us what Dan said?" asks Officer Sahin.

I am so relieved that she has understood. "YES," I sniff. "THEY WONT CATCH ME."

I can't believe I have managed to say a whole sentence. Suddenly, I remember the knife. I didn't tell Mom that.

I sniff quickly before Officer Sahin can ask another question.

"KNIFE." Is that clear? She looks unsure, but Dad's eyes light up.

"I think I know what Jemma means... Can I...?" Dad begins.

"I'd rather we ask the questions if you don't mind. We have to make sure we don't ask anything leading," says Officer Hunt.

"Oh, okay," says Dad.

"You know something about a knife?" Officer Sahin asks me. "Can you tell me more about it?"

"OLIVIA KNIFE," I sniff.

Officer Hunt looks confused. I'm not explaining clearly enough. I wish I could talk more in whole sentences, but sniffing each letter is so much effort.

Dad can see I'm struggling, and he ignores Officer Hunt's

request to keep quiet. "Olivia found a knife in our garden," he says. "I'll get it."

I hear his footsteps leave and come back a few moments later. "Here."

I can't see because of the angle, but I assume Dad is giving Officer Hunt the knife. I hear the rustle of plastic. "Just put it straight in here," says Officer Hunt.

"KNIFE RYAN," I sniff.

"Does it look like the kind of knife that stabbed Ryan?" Dad asks.

"I couldn't comment on that," says Officer Hunt.

"DANS KNIFE," I sniff.

"Do you know that?" Officer Hunt asks.

"THINK," I admit.

"Jemma, when did Dan tell you he killed Ryan?"

There's a tone in his voice as if he's not sure he believes me.

When did he tell me? I can't remember! It was weeks ago. Is it okay to say that?

"WEEKS AGO," I sniff. I feel I need to explain more, although it is taking a lot of effort.

"Do you know anything about Sarah's disappearance?" Officer Sahin asks.

What can I say? "DAN," I sniff.

"You know Dan is responsible—or you think he might be?"

"THINK," I sniff.

"Do you know of any reason why Dan might be responsible?"

"RICHARD," I sniff.

Officer Sahin nods thoughtfully.

All the energy has drained from me. I need a break. I hope there are not too many more questions.

"TIRED," I sniff.

"Okay," says Officer Sahin. "I think that's enough questions for now."

"What happens next?" Dad asks. "I mean, Jemma can't sign a statement or anything."

"We'll need you to bring Jemma to the station so we can film her answering these questions," Officer Sahin explains. "The video evidence can be used in court if needed. You have been very helpful, Jemma—very helpful indeed."

"Good job, dear," says Mom, stroking my arm.

"TIRED," I sniff again.

"You look washed out," Mom says, stroking my cheek. She turns to Officer Sahin. "I really don't think she can answer all these questions again now."

"How about you rest and come to the station after lunch?" Officer Sahin suggests.

"Thank you, we'll do that," says Mom.

"GET DAN," I sniff.

"We'll certainly be making further inquiries," Officer Sahin assures me.

I've done it! I've told them—although I wish I didn't have to do it all over again for the video. At least they are taking me seriously. The police will arrest Dan, and they'll find out what happened to Sarah. I feel ecstatic at being able to communicate something so important. "Do you want to lie down?" Mom asks when they've gone.

"YES," I sniff.

"It's so nice to be able to ask you what you want rather than decide for you," she says as she wheels me into my bedroom.

But lying there on my bed, I couldn't sleep. My head felt like it was full of bees buzzing around and around. I couldn't switch off until I knew the police had locked Dan up.

I heard Mr. Fogel leave and wished I'd said goodbye to him and told him how grateful I was—though I could hear Mom and Dad thanking him again and again.

By the time I'd been to the police station with Mom and gone through all the questions again, I felt like I had nothing left. I wish I'd managed to ask if they'd arrested Dan yet, but answering the questions had used up all my energy.

As we left the police station, we passed a police car arriving. Maybe Dan was in it. I wish I could have seen. Back home, I was able to ask to lie down again.

Mom took out the sniff controller tube, and that time I fell asleep instantly.

Now I'm awake, and I have no idea how much time has

passed. I can hear Mom's voice. I think she's in the kitchen on the phone. I try to listen, but I can't hear what Mom's saying or figure out who she's talking to. Is it the police?

Mom doesn't come. I'm lying here, waiting and waiting.

Finally her head appears around the door.

"I was feeling impatient, wondering what was happening," she tells me, "so I called the station." She smiles. "They've got him, Jemma! The police have got Dan. They're questioning him now."

I'm so relieved. *They've got him!* I wish I could have seen his face when he opened the door for them.

But what about Sarah?

Mom sits me up gently and moves me into my wheelchair. She pushes me into the living room before connecting the sniff controller. It takes a few tries to get the tube up my nose right. "We'll get some kind of clamp so we can attach the tablet to your chair," she tells me as she props it up on a tray so I can see it. I am impatient, eager to ask about Sarah.

"SARAH?" I finally sniff.

"No news yet," says Mom, "but give them a chance, Jemma. Would you like a drink? I'm going to make myself a cup of tea."

"WATER," I sniff. It still feels incredible to be able to ask for things.

I think about Dan, imagining him being questioned. I hope he's squirming in his chair, stuck for words. I'd love for him to know what it's like when you can't speak. I hope he's scared too—really scared.

Mom brings the drinks, sits down near me, and helps me drink the water from a straw.

"It must have been terrible for you," she says as she sips her tea, "knowing all that and not being able to tell us."

"YES," I sniff slowly.

"And we were all taken in by him, apart from you."

"YES," I sniff. Though I know if I had been able to talk, Dan would never have shared his secret with me.

"SARAH?" I ask again after dinner.

"I'll phone the station and see if there's any update," Mom tells me.

"WANT," I sniff.

"What do you want, Jemma?" she asks. "HEAR," I continue.

"Of course," says Mom. She fiddles with the phone, turning on the speaker.

I wait while Mom gets through to Officer Hunt.

"We wondered if there was any news about Sarah," Mom says.

"Well," says Officer Hunt, "we've talked to Dan Harris, but unfortunately we've found no reason to hold him."

"Oh?" says Mom.

"He has an alibi for the evening Ryan was killed, and we have no other evidence against him. There is nothing to indicate he is connected with Sarah's disappearance either. He has an alibi for that night too. So we've had to let him go."

"Goodness," says Mom.

My breath comes fast. I don't believe it. The police have

made a mistake. Dan must've lied about his alibis. I know he did it. I know!

"But Jemma was so sure," Mom says quietly. "I don't believe she was making it up."

"It wasn't exactly your average witness statement," Officer Hunt says. "She's never spoken before. Maybe she got overexcited, started making up stories. Maybe it's all jumbled in her head."

He doesn't believe a word I said! He'd rather believe Dan. *Making up stories...jumbled in her head.* How dare he say that?

Mom glances at me, and I think she's wishing she hadn't put the speaker on. I hope she doesn't turn it off now.

"TRUE," I sniff to Mom. "WAS DAN."

"I think Jemma believed what she told you to be true," Mom tells Officer Hunt. "Dan may have been joking with her, but I'm sure Jemma heard what she says she heard."

"You know her best, of course, but like I said—it's a weird situation. Perhaps she just wanted something dramatic to say. She's a teenager, after all."

Even Mom is speechless at this. I can speak, but I don't know what to say either.

"What about the knife?" Mom suddenly asks. "Was it the one that killed Ryan?"

"The knife will be tested," Officer Hunt tells her.

"And Sarah?" asks Mom.

"Sarah remains on the missing persons list. Hopefully, in time she will make contact. We'll keep you informed."

Mom gets off the phone and looks at me. "Are you all right, Jemma?"

I am seething. I want this tube out of my nose, but I don't feel like sniffing, not even to say that. How can he have an alibi? It must be a lie. Why can't the police see through him? They'd rather believe him than me—just because I'm in a wheelchair and he's standing on his own two feet. I know I'm right. The way Officer Hunt spoke about me was utterly humiliating.

"Jemma?" Mom asks again.

I don't answer. I'm not sniffing again, not ever.

I have nothing more to say.

48

"Jemma's had a shock," *I* hear Mom saying. It's the next morning, and she's on the phone to Mr. Fogel. "I'm not sure if she's stopped trying to sniff or whether the sniff controller has stopped working," she tells him. There's a pause. "Okay," Mom says. "I'll contact you in a few days. We'll see what happens. Thank you."

Mom has to realize. She doesn't really think it's broken, does she?

At breakfast Dad tries to encourage me to speak. I don't. I won't. Breakfast is very quiet. No Sarah and no Olivia either. I miss her. In a weird way, I even miss her tantrums.

After breakfast, Finn has his box of matchsticks and is lining them up against the kitchen wall when he accidentally steps on the box and the matches spill. He is horrified, frantically trying to pick them up and put them back, but he's trying to do it too fast and some of them spill out again.

This is how I feel—like everything's spilling out, all over

the place. Like Finn, I want life to all be straight lines for a change.

"Here, let me help you, Finn," Dad says gently. Finn doesn't react, but he doesn't stop Dad either. Soon the matches are all back in the box, and Finn goes back to lining them up.

"Jemma," Dad says, sitting beside me and touching my arm. "You told the police what you knew. It isn't your fault that Dan lied to you. What he did was very unkind."

Unkind. I still can't believe it was a lie—not when I think about what he said when he learned there might be a way for me to communicate.

"Don't let that spoil things. You can talk to us, Jemma! It's incredible. Don't let Dan or the police take that away."

They're not taking it away. I just don't want to do it anymore. That's all.

By the evening there is no further news, and I am still not sniffing. Dad phones Kate, but she has nothing to report.

"Talk to me, Jemma," Mom begs as she clears up from dinner. "Tell me how you're feeling. I know it must be tough."

She has no idea how tough. And no, I'm not talking, not to anyone.

"What would cheer you up?" Mom asks.

Dan in prison, finding Sarah, everything getting back to normal—but that's not going to happen, is it? Nothing will cheer me up.

By bedtime I have still not sniffed at all.

"What about Jodi?" Mom suggests gently, putting an arm around my shoulder. "Would you like to see her?" My sister. I don't feel like talking, but maybe...

Jodi. That's different. Now that Mom has said it, I know she's right. Mom has said the only thing that might possibly make me feel a little better.

But she's given up on waiting for me to answer. She stands up to walk out of the room.

"YES," I sniff.

49

I am waiting for Jodi. Yesterday passed so slowly, and now she's late and I'm scared she's changed her mind. Apart from sniffing "YES" to seeing Jodi, I have kept quiet. Dad has attached the tablet to my wheelchair with a clamp so I can speak whenever I want to, but I still don't feel like talking. I'm not even sure I'm going to talk to Jodi. I want to see her, though.

We wait. Where is she? She was supposed to be here half an hour ago.

Mom looks at her watch. "I'll text her in a minute if she still hasn't arrived," she tells me.

Then I hear the bell, and Mom goes to answer the door.

"Hi, Jodi," I hear her say.

"So sorry I'm late!" Jodi replies.

"Don't worry. Jemma will be delighted that you're here," says Mom. "Come in."

"I'm a little nervous," I hear Jodi say. "This sniff thing...

How does it work? Will I need to do anything?" I don't want Jodi to be nervous.

"It's easy," says Mom. "Jemma does it all! We'll show you. She might not say much, though."

Finally they come in from the hallway. Mom points Jodi toward the sofa.

She turns me so I'll be facing Jodi, who sits down a little awkwardly.

"Hi, Jemma. So sorry I'm late! The bus took *forever*. The traffic was terrible."

"I'll get you a drink," Mom tells her. "What would you like? Tea? Coke?"

"Coke, please," says Jodi.

Mom goes out. Jodi leans toward me. "Now, show me how this thing works," she says. "I'm so excited that you can speak!"

Her excitement is infectious. My wonderful sister is here, and I can talk to her. I want to... I really do.

"HAPPY," I sniff slowly.

"Wow! That's so cool," she says, watching patiently as the letters appear and the voice finally speaks. "I'm so happy to see you too, Jemma!"

There's an awkward pause. I guess it's my turn to speak. What do I say? My mind goes blank.

Maybe Jodi will say something else—but she doesn't. I have to say something. Now I understand what Professor

Spalding meant about learning to speak. Even though I can think clearly and my thoughts just come into my head with no effort, with speech I have to decide what to say and choose the words. And then with AAC I need to find the shortest words, to use the least effort to express what I want to say. I feel panicky. I say the only thing that comes into my head.

"SAD SARAH," I tell Jodi. It takes me a long time to get all this out.

"Sarah's sad? No, you're sad about Sarah? You must miss her so much."

"YES," I sniff. Jodi gets it—she understands me! There's another pause. Jodi's not saying anything.

I realize I should ask her something, but I can't think what.

"Actually, I've had quite a week myself," she tells me. "I broke up with Jack. We'd only been going out for a month, but I really liked him. He went off with another girl from my class."

"IDIOT," I sniff, and Jodi bursts out laughing. It's awesome that I can make her laugh.

"NEW BOY," I sniff.

Jodi smiles. "I need a new boyfriend? Yes, actually there is a boy I've got my eye on... He's a year older than me."

"GOOD LUCK," I sniff.

"Ha! Thanks!" Jodi grins. "I'll let you know how it goes! Is there anyone you like, Jemma?"

I am about to sniff *no* but then I remember.

Actually, there is.

"LEO GLOWLIGHT," I tell her.

"You like Glowlight too! You're right. He's awesome!"
Jodi laughs.

A strange snort comes from my throat. I think I am
actually laughing too!

"LOVE YOU JODI," I sniff.

"I love you too, Jemma," Jodi tells me. "It's so cool that we
can really talk now!"

Mom comes back with a Coke for Jodi and an apple juice
for me. She's taken a while—maybe she was just giving us
some time to talk. She puts the straw in my cup and holds it up.

"I can do that," says Jodi.

"I'll leave you to it, then," says Mom, smiling. "Just call
me if you need anything."

Mom's gone. Jodi holds my cup and eases the straw into
my mouth. I sip.

She puts the drink down. She is quiet again. I'm tired
from all the sniffing, but I don't want to stop. I'm just not sure
what to say.

"FIND SARAH," I sniff.

"It must be awful not knowing what's happened," says
Jodi. She strokes my hand. "I wish there was something I could
do to help, but I think you'll have to leave it to the police."

"NO GOOD," I tell her.

She laughs. "It's their job. I'm sure they're trying their
best."

"WE FIND HER," I sniff. "YOU ME."

"But...how?"

"TRY," I sniff.

"Okay, then." Jodi sighs and leans forward. "You must've known Sarah so well, better than anyone, maybe. Think about everything you know, Jemma. Tell me if you can think of anything—*anything*—at all that might help."

I think hard. I love it that Jodi is listening. But what do I know that I haven't already told the police?

"SARAH LOVE DAN," I sniff. I'm pleased that I'm already getting faster at it, though it still takes me a long time.

"Okay..." Jodi says, frowning.

"DAN BAD MAN," I sniff.

"But he didn't kill Ryan," says Jodi.

"DID," I sniff. "AND HE GOT SARAH."

"Come on, then." Jodi smiles. "How are we going to prove it? What else do you know?"

I try to remember everything I know about Dan, every time that he came to the house. The things he said to me flash through my head, making me shudder. What do I know that could help? There has to be something, but I just can't think.

Jodi sits waiting, fiddling with a pretty ring on her finger. Her phone starts buzzing. She looks at it and switches it off. "Nothing important," she says, smiling. I have a sudden memory—Dan standing here, his cell phone ringing. Billy—it was Billy. Could he know something?

"DAN FRIEND BILLY," I sniff.

"Do the police know about him?" Jodi asks.

"NO," I sniff. I don't know for certain, but I don't think so.

"What do you know about Billy?" she asks.

I remember what Sarah called him. "BILLY NO BRAINS."

Jodi laughs. "Oh yeah?"

"BIG HEAD BIG BRAIN?"

"Big heads don't always equal big brains, Jemma." Jodi laughs.

"DAN PHONE BILLY," I continue.

"You heard him? What did he say?"

I try to remember. It wasn't anything that interesting, or it would have stuck in my mind. Then it comes to me. "BEHIND THE GROCERY."

"Interesting," says Jodi. "What do you think he meant was behind the grocery store?"

"DONT KNOW," I sniff. This is hard work. I can't keep sniffing like this. It's wearing me out. But then I have another thought. "YOU ME GO."

"Go where?"

"STORE," I sniff. "NOT FAR."

"You really think this might be important?"

"YES."

Jodi smiles at me. "Okay, then."

50

She goes into the kitchen and asks Mom if she can take me for a walk. Mom sounds pleased, and a minute later she comes in with my coat.

"Don't be out too long. It still gets dark so early. Oh, and if you pass the grocery store, would you mind picking up a few onions for me?" Mom asks her. "Here, I'll give you the money."

"Sure," says Jodi. "I've never pushed a wheelchair before," she adds, suddenly sounding nervous. I hope she's not going to change her mind.

"Jemma's well strapped in," Mom tells her. "Going up and down curbs is the only tricky thing. Come outside, and I'll give you a demo."

Soon we are off! I am out with my sister. I jerk the first couple of times we go down a curb, but then Jodi gets the hang of it. She seems to be enjoying it. She starts to run, pushing me fast so the wind zooms past my face. This is great!

I direct her to the grocery store so we can get Mom's onions there and investigate. Left, then second right. Then all the way to the other end of the block and left. She stops at each junction, and I tell her which way to go. It's not complicated, but I hope I'm doing it right. I've only been there a couple of times—and I've never given directions before.

To my relief, the store comes into view. This part of town is kind of run-down and dingy. There are some row houses, but it's mostly apartment buildings, warehouses, and office complexes. Some of the buildings look derelict and have boarded-up windows. Others have scaffolding around them. There are very few people around. I start to feel nervous. The tablet attached to my wheelchair might look very tempting to a thief. And I got so carried away with the idea of coming here that I didn't actually think about what we'd do when we got here.

Jodi stops outside the store. "What now, Jemma?" I don't know what to say. Jodi turns me right and left so I can see in both directions. It doesn't help much. Jodi stops, and I stare at the door, thinking. Then I remember what Dan said. "BEHIND," I sniff.

"Okay, here we go," she says.

Around the back, there are dumpsters. Lots of dumpsters. Some of them are overflowing.

"Hmmm," says Jodi. She turns me slowly so I can see all the way around.

There is the delivery entrance, a few spaces for cars to park. Not much else that could hold a clue.

"Should we go?" Jodi asks me.

I am about to sniff "YES." This was a stupid idea, and I wish we'd never come. What Dan said to Billy was the only thing I could remember, and I thought it might mean something. That was ridiculous, wasn't it? But I am reluctant to leave.

"TURN," I say.

"Okay."

Again Jodi turns me. There's a passageway between two tall buildings. It looks dark and uninviting, but I think we should investigate. It's hard for me to get Jodi to stop in the right place so she'll see where I mean.

"Well?" she asks.

"TURN," I repeat.

She turns me twice more, and I am starting to feel dizzy before we are finally pointing in the right direction.

"THAT WAY," I sniff.

"Okay," she says. "We'll have a look, and then we'll go." The buildings tower above us as Jodi pushes me along the alley between them, their flat roofs merging with the gray-black of the late-afternoon sky. I feel very small. There is no sidewalk, so I hope no cars choose this moment to enter. We come out into a narrow yard with a row of run-down garages. A few have closed doors, but some doors are hanging off and some garages have no doors at all. The nearest open one has stacks of bricks inside, and another has a pile of wooden planks.

Jodi pushes me nearer. There is a smell like dirty toilets. It's getting darker too.

"I don't like it here," says Jodi. "Can we go now?"

I don't like it here either, but I'm reluctant to leave. I can't exactly ask Jodi to look in those creepy garages. "YES," I tell her. "SORRY."

"It's okay," she says. "It was worth a look, if you thought it might be important. I'm not sure what we were looking for, though."

She is pushing me back toward the passage when I hear a sound behind us—a clang of metal. Jodi doesn't seem to hear, and I can't turn to look. We're moving so I can't tell her to stop. It was probably nothing.

We're nearly at the gap between the buildings when I hear voices—men's voices. They're coming from the alley we are heading to—and they are getting closer. Jodi instinctively pulls me back and around the side of the garages so they won't see us. I suddenly feel very vulnerable. What if they find us?

I want to know what's happening, but Jodi doesn't dare risk putting her head out in case she is seen. I hope I can keep quiet. I can't help making sounds sometimes. The more I think about trying to keep quiet, the more I worry that a sound will come out. I try not to think about it, to focus on listening as the voices come nearer.

"I don't like it," says one man. "It's gone on too long." The voice sounds familiar. It could be Billy. It sounds like him, though the tone is anxious, not relaxed like when I met him. It could easily be a stranger.

"Quit whining," says another voice.

That's Dan. Now I'm sure it's Billy too. I can barely breathe.

"You've gotta let her go, man!" says Billy, pleadingly. "We can't just keep her..."

"I told you to shut up! I'll figure it out, okay?" says Dan.

"What do you mean?" says Billy.

"Don't know why you're scared after what you..." I don't catch the end of the sentence. They're moving away from us now. I hear the clink of keys.

Then the sound of one of the garage doors lifting and going down again.

I've got to get Jodi to call the police. She's got to do it quickly. But my breathing's gone all weird, and I can't sniff. I get a surge of panic.

Jodi whispers to me. "Is that them? Were they talking about Sarah?"

"YES." The word appears on the screen, but I am careful not to select the speaker button. It's hard to sniff accurately. I have to slow down, even though I want to get the words out fast. "POLICE."

I can see Jodi hesitating. Maybe she's wondering if it's safe to call from here, or if it is even more dangerous to move in case they come out and spot us.

Jodi takes out her cell phone. "Police," she says quietly when the call connects. There's another pause. "We think someone's being held prisoner. Behind the grocery store on Redding Road, in one of the derelict garages. We're too scared to move. Two of us. My sister's in a wheelchair." She listens, then hangs up.

"They're coming," she whispers.

I'm starting to feel shivery. *What if Dan heard?*

What if he finds us here?

We wait. The buildings around us seem to creak and groan. Apart from that, it is quiet. Did the police believe Jodi? Did they realize the urgency?

At last! There is the crunch of tires and the sound of an engine. The police car pauses at our end of the gap, headlights lighting the gray alley. Jodi runs out. I can't see what's happening. I hear the car doors opening, footsteps.

There's a muffled scream—a woman's scream. Then I hear the voice.

"Police!"

I hear shouting, banging. I'm terrified. I can't see Jodi. I can't see anything. The police car is in the way.

It feels like forever, and my heart is thudding like a drum. What's happening? *What?*

Then I hear the voice again. "Ambulance needed, garages on Redding Road, behind the grocery store."

A gurgling noise comes from my throat. *No!* Then I hear, "Woman in her twenties, conscious but injured."

She's alive! Sarah's alive!

Jodi is back. She pushes me out into the open, which is now action-packed, like something from a movie. There are more flashing lights. A police van is here now too. A man is in handcuffs, being put in the back. I can't see well, but I think it's Billy.

"Move back," a policeman tells us. Then suddenly Dan is in front of me. He's handcuffed too. His eyes meet mine. His mouth drops open in astonishment.

I feel hot and cold all at once. *I got you, Dan. I got you!*

And then I realize I can say something. At last, I can say something to Dan. I start to sniff.

"FREAK."

Dan's shoulders jolt in surprise, and his eyes are wide. He turns away, and the policeman blocks my view as Dan's put into the van. An ambulance arrives, and there is hardly space for it to park. The paramedics jump out, and I wait. I desperately want to see Sarah. But she doesn't appear. They're taking forever. How badly hurt is she? The police are saying we should go home. A policeman offers to come with us, but Jodi says no, it's not far to walk. They say they'll take statements from us later. They are talking to Jodi as if I am not there.

"We came because of Jemma," Jodi says. "Something she

overheard. She thought it might be important and wanted to check it out."

"Well, it was a really risky thing to do," says the police officer, "but you did well, both of you."

When we reach home, Jodi rings the bell and Mom opens the door, smiling. "You were gone a while. Everything okay?"

Jodi doesn't speak. I think the shock of everything has suddenly hit her.

"Did you manage to get the onions?" asks Mom.

"NO," I sniff. "GOT DAN."

"You did what?" Mom asks as we make our way into the kitchen.

"We forgot the onions, but the police have Dan," Jodi tells Mom. "Because of Jemma."

Mom's mouth opens, but she can't speak.

"FOUND SARAH," I tell her.

"Is she...?" Mom asks.

"She's alive," says Jodi.

Mom listens to our story. A police officer arrives at the door. I recognize him from the garages. He says he is Detective Sergeant Bell, and he wants to ask me and Jodi some questions. He wants us to come to the station so they can videotape my answers. I have done so much sniffing today that I can barely stay awake. I ask how Sarah is, but all the detective can say is that she's been taken to the hospital, which I already know.

At least at the police station Sergeant Bell questions me as if he believes everything I'm saying. He's very different from Officer Hunt.

When we're finished, Mom drops Jodi off at her house and takes me home. I am able to tell her I want to sit in the living room with some gentle music on. I think if she hadn't been able to ask me, she would have put me to bed, but my mind is whirring far too much to sleep.

I can't believe what just happened. What Dan did... It makes me sick. Keeping Sarah locked up in a garage all these weeks, and coming around here pretending he was worried about her. And what if Jodi and I hadn't been there at that moment? I think how we nearly turned back. We were about to. I shudder. Poor Sarah... I can't imagine what it was like locked in there. She must have been desperate. She must have wondered if she'd ever get out.

Then I think about what I did. I can hardly believe that either. Dan thought I was powerless, but I wasn't. I knew I wanted to communicate, but I never really thought about the power it would give me. I feel different—as if I have a new inner strength. Even so, I realize there are some things you just can't control—no one can—like the way other people behave.

———

We have fish and french fries for dinner, and I manage to sniff, "KETCHUP." Mom looks at me in surprise before mashing some ketchup into my fries. Mom fills Dad in on everything that's happened. Dad shakes his head in disbelief.

I watch Finn lining up his fries in neat rows on his plate. The next minute, he's pushed the plate away and is banging his head on the table.

"Finn! Stop that," Dad tells him. "What's the matter?"

I look, and I can see what's wrong. Finn is one fry short. As he leaned over the plate, a fry attached itself to his sweater and is still hanging below his elbow.

I have to swallow my mouthful, and then I sniff, "FINN."

His head jerks up in surprise at the computer voice saying his name. He looks bewildered. He doesn't seem sure where it's coming from.

I select the speaker again. "FINN. FINN." Until he looks at me. "FRY SWEATER," I tell him. Finn looks at his sweater and suddenly sees the french fry. He pulls it off and puts it back in line on his plate.

"Nice job, Jemma," says Dad.

This is the first thing I have said to Finn. He glances up at me, meeting my eyes for just a second. He's smiling.

The next day Mom is supposed to come with me to school to show my teachers how the sniff controller works. I feel completely drained after yesterday, though, and tell her I don't feel up to going to school.

"Don't worry," says Mom. "Stay home today and rest. I'll come and show them another day."

It is late afternoon when the phone rings. Mom answers it and then runs into the living room.

"Jemma, that was Paula. The police have gotten the DNA results back from the knife. Someone tried to clean it with bleach, apparently, but there were still tiny specks of blood. It was the knife that killed Ryan!"

"DAN," I sniff.

"No," says Mom. "Dan's alibi for that night was backed up by security cameras. He was miles away at a casino, or something. But what they have discovered is that a hair found on Ryan's clothing belongs to Billy. He's the main suspect now, Paula says."

"WHY BILLY," I sniff. That doesn't make sense.

If Billy killed Ryan, why did Dan make me think he did it?

"I've no idea why Billy did it," says Mom.

"SARAH?" I ask.

"I've spoken to Kate," says Mom. "They're keeping her in the hospital for a few days, but it sounds like she'll be okay."

I am so relieved. I just want her back here.

52

Sarah is coming! There's been a weird atmosphere at home these last few days—such a mixture of things, like one of Mom's "everything goes in" stews. We're all pleased and relieved that Sarah's been found, that she's alive—but shocked too, and horrified at what she's been through. I am less shocked than Mom and Dad because I knew what Dan was like, but I still feel dreadful thinking about all those days Sarah was locked in that garage. If I only I could have told them sooner, if only I could have warned Sarah, she might not have had to go through all that.

Kate wanted Sarah to go and stay with her, but Sarah wanted to come here. I am worried about what state she'll be in, how she'll be feeling, but I can't wait for her to be back. Once Sarah is here, things will feel a little more normal again.

I hear the bell. My heart starts beating so fast.

Sarah. *Sarah!* But the voice isn't Sarah's. It's Paula.

"Jemma," says Paula, as she comes into the living room. "Thank you so much! It's because of you that they got him, that evil man."

"Do they know why did Billy did it?" Mom asks her.

"He's a thief," Paula tells us. "The police have connected him to a string of thefts from jewelers. I suspected my Ryan had gotten himself into some kind of a mess. They think he was helping out with raids and decided to keep some of the stuff himself. And Billy found out."

Mom is shaking her head as she takes all this in.

Paula keeps talking. "And I'm thinking that if Dan knew what Billy had done, he might have used it to make Billy help him kidnap Sarah."

There's a pause as all of this sinks in. "SARAH COMING," I sniff.

"Really?" says Paula. "That's wonderful! The poor girl. It's dreadful to think..."

"Yes, she should be here soon," Mom says, looking at her watch. "It's because of Jemma that they found Sarah too, of course."

Mom smiles at me.

"Anyway, I won't stick around if you're expecting Sarah," Paula says, standing up. "I just wanted to fill you in—and to thank you, Jemma. I'll be off."

Paula has only been gone two minutes when the doorbell rings again.

So many times I've imagined her walking through the door. And here she is.

I knew she might look different after going through something so horrific, but this doesn't stop the shock when I see her. She looks thinner. Her hair is lank, her skin spotty, and her eyes have a scary emptiness. She does manage a tiny smile when she sees me. She opens her mouth as if to speak, but she coughs. The cough is chesty and hollow, and it sounds like it will never stop.

"Jemma, it's so good to see you," she finally croaks. "Thank you...for everything." Her voice is sad and small, and even though I know she's pleased to see me, it feels as though part of her is somewhere else.

Now is my chance—my chance to communicate with Sarah for the first time. "LOVE YOU SARAH," I sniff.

She manages a slightly bigger smile. "Wow. Look at you talking!"

There's a silence. No one really knows what to say. She knows—she must know—we care about her so much. But you can't just fix something like this.

Sarah turns to Mom. "I'll go and have a shower, if that's okay," she says. "I had showers at the hospital of course, but I don't feel clean. I can't..."

"Have a shower, dear. Take as long as you want," says Mom.

She disappears upstairs. It is Sarah, but it isn't. Things aren't going to be the same. And of course I knew that, deep down. It will be good that I can speak, though. I want to help her feel better.

Sarah doesn't come down for about an hour. I wait and wait. She looks better, but her face still has an emptiness.

"Cup of tea?" asks Mom.

"Thank you." Sarah nods.

Mom goes into the kitchen to make it, and Sarah sits down with me.

"I can't believe I was so wrong about him," she says quietly. "I guess you knew, Jemma. I bet you've got more sense than me."

"I KNEW," I tell her.

"I should have stuck with Richard, sweet Richard. I don't know what got into me."

Mom comes in at the end of this. "Dan was a charmer," she says. "Anyone can fall for a charmer."

"He said I was his and his alone, like he owned me." Sarah looks shaky.

"Don't talk about it now unless you want to," says Mom, touching Sarah's shoulder gently.

Sarah takes a sip of tea and then coughs that chesty cough again.

"Have they given you something for that cough?" Mom asks.

Sarah nods. "I've got antibiotics. It was freezing and drafty in that garage."

"How could he do it—treat you like that?" Mom's voice
is bitter. "He deceived us all, you know."

I wasn't taken in, but I don't bother to point this out.

"You're welcome to stay here and rest up," says Mom.
"Take all the time you need to recover. It must've been a
horrendous ordeal."

"Thanks," says Sarah. She rubs her eyes. "Look, I don't...
This, this is so hard... I hope you'll all understand, but..."

I brace myself as Sarah pauses. But *what*?

Sarah sighs. "I need space and time to figure things out.
I wanted to come here because this is my home, but I'm
only staying a few days. Then I'll go to my sister's. I need
time to think."

"WANT YOU STAY," I sniff. "I LOOK AFTER YOU."

Sarah gives a little gasp. "That is so sweet, Jemma. I love
you. This... It's nothing to do with you, I promise. I don't
know. I just need space."

As I try to take in this awful news, Sarah tells us that
Richard visited her in hospital yesterday.

"He feels so bad about not seeing me go into the house
after the concert," she says. "I tried to say he's got nothing to
feel bad about... I was cheating on him!"

"I don't think you or Richard should worry yourselves
about that now, not after everything." Mom sighs. "What
happened when you got out of the car after the concert?"
she asks. Then she puts her hand over her mouth. "I'm

sorry, I shouldn't have asked. I'm sure you don't want to talk about it."

"It's okay," says Sarah. "I got to the front door, and just as I went to put the key in, a hand went over my mouth. Dan was holding me tight, forcing me to walk, and he bundled me into a car and drove me to that garage. He'd found out about Richard, and he was angry—so angry! But I deserved it, didn't I?" Sarah breaks into sobs.

"You can't think that!" says Mom, just as I sniff, "NO."

"Dan may have felt angry, but that could never make it okay—what he did," says Mom. Her fists are clenched.

Sarah bursts into tears. Mom is by her side in a second. She puts her arm around Sarah and grabs some tissues from the table. I try to think of something I can say.

But I guess sometimes there is nothing you can say.

It's just being there that's important.

I can't take in that she's leaving. Is she going to come back? I have wanted her back so much. I know the most important thing is that she's okay—and that she does what she needs to do right now. I'm trying not to think about myself in this, but I don't want her to go, not now. Not right away.

Later, I am lying in bed and overhear Mom and Dad talking in the kitchen. Sarah has gone to bed early.

"I can't stand thinking about it," Mom says. "Her being locked up in that garage all that time. At least she says he didn't lay a finger on her."

"No, just left her there to rot," Dad says sourly.

"Acted like he was doing her a favor by bringing a little bit of food and water. Expecting her to be grateful... Can you imagine?" says Mom. "I'm not surprised she wants a break."

"Maybe we need a break too," Dad says. I feel a flash of alarm. What is he saying?

"We've had such a tough few months," Dad continues. "Jemma could go to that college. I'm sure she'll do well now she has the sniff controller. Someone else could take Finn."

"No!" says Mom.

I am relieved that she sounds so horrified.

"You know how he hates change—and Jemma too," says Mom. "They need us."

"We're only good for them if we are in a good state ourselves. And I'm not sure we are," says Dad.

Then I hear Mom crying.

I knew things weren't going to stay the same, but Mom and Dad? I thought they'd always be here. How wrong could I be?

53

All night, my mind tosses and turns even though my body can't. I thought my world was going to be back to normal now that Dan is in custody. I thought my home, my "nest," would be safe—with Mom and Dad and Sarah and Finn and the chance to get to know my sister Jodi too.

I can speak. I told Mom to let Olivia stay, and they've sent her away. I told Sarah I wanted her to stay and I love her—but it made no difference. So what is the point?

I am awake when Mom comes to turn me. I realize Sarah may never do it again—never turn me, never read to me, never paint my nails, never confide her secrets. In the morning, Mom puts my sniff-controller tubes up my nose, but I have nothing to say. I can't stand what's happening, and I don't even answer when Mom asks me if I am okay. Sarah doesn't come down for breakfast. Mom takes up a tray with coffee and toast.

"Talk to me, Jemma," Mom says gently when she comes

down. "You can tell me how you feel and what you're thinking now. Let me try to help."

I know I am being mean, but I don't feel like communicating. It is an effort to do it, and I don't even know what to say.

"Are you upset about Sarah?" Mom asks me.

I rouse myself to sniff *Y* and then select *YES* from the predictive text.

"I know," says Mom. "We got her back, and now she's going again. It's so hard, isn't it? But we'll get by. This is what she needs—and whatever happens, she's part of our family. And we'll make sure you always have the care you need, Jemma."

She's looking at me as if she's waiting for a response. I want to ask, "Are you going to stop fostering?" but I'm too scared. What if she says yes?

I watch as Mom empties the dishwasher. I feel like I have been emptied too.

"Come on, I'm taking you somewhere," says Mom.

"WHERE," I sniff.

"Wait and see," says Mom.

I am soon in the car with Mom. I want to know where we're going. We drive for about ten minutes. I am shocked when she parks outside the police station. I can't believe there are more questions. I've told the police everything I know. Mom lowers the ramp and wheels me out of the car, pushing me toward the entrance.

"WHY HERE," I sniff. "GO HOME."

"You'll see," says Mom.

Mom speaks to the woman behind the screen, and a police officer comes out.

"Mrs. Bryant! Jemma! I'm so glad you're here."

I recognize his voice before he comes around in front so I can see him. It's Officer Hunt, the one who said I invented my story. He's the last person I want to see. He may be glad I'm here, but I'm not.

"Come this way," he says.

"NO," I sniff, but Mom ignores me. Officer Hunt smiles at her as he holds a door open and she pushes me through.

He's got nothing to smile about as far as I'm concerned.

He leads us into a room and moves a chair aside to make room for my wheelchair. He holds a chair out for Mom and then sits down opposite us and strokes his chin.

"GO HOME," I sniff.

"I can understand why you're not eager to be here," says Officer Hunt. "But I asked your mom to bring you for a reason. I have something important to say to you."

I had something important to say to you last week, I think. *But look how that turned out.*

"I wanted to apologize to you, face-to-face," he says. He's looking straight into my eyes, and he looks serious. "This crime has been solved thanks to you. I know you heard some things I said on the phone to your mom, things I should never have said. I'm sorry if I upset you."

"YOU DID," I sniff. I'm not letting him off that easily.

He smiles awkwardly. "You found Sarah—and Dan and Billy are locked up now, thanks to your help."

"I SAID DAN," I remind him. "NO LISTEN."

"Yes, you were right—and in more ways than you know."

What does he mean? I am interested now. "Although Dan didn't actually kill Ryan Blake," he goes on, "we now believe Dan got Billy to do it for him."

I begin to sniff. "DAN MADE."

Officer Hunt nods. "Exactly. Dan made Billy do it. Billy has finally agreed to help us with our investigation. He says he was working for Dan, and Ryan was too. He told us that when Dan found out Ryan was keeping some of the stolen goods, he was furious. He wasn't going to allow it—and told Billy to kill him."

"Sounds like Dan was a complete control freak," says Mom. "And yet he could be so charming..."

Officer Hunt nods solemnly. "Billy is not the brightest guy around. Dan had him wrapped around his finger. Billy admits that he panicked after stabbing Ryan and went running to Dan, who took the knife and said he'd deal with it. He must've been visiting Sarah and took the opportunity to stash it in your backyard. We've charged Dan with conspiracy to murder."

"I'm just glad you've got him," says Mom, "and Billy too."

"Jemma," says Officer Hunt. "I'm sorry I didn't believe you. I was wrong."

I am shocked. He actually means it.

"But you didn't give up. You were determined to prove your theory right. And you did! We'll do our best to make sure Dan and Billy are both locked up for a long time. I hope you can forgive me, Jemma."

I am stunned. I don't know what to say. His eyes look desperate now, pleading with me to let him off the hook. I didn't think he cared, but now I believe he does.

"OKAY," I sniff.

"Thank you," he says, his shoulders sinking with clear relief. "That means a lot."

54

I've realized something important. Being able to communicate doesn't mean that anyone's going to listen. The one thing I didn't want to have happen is happening, and there is nothing I can say to stop it.

"I know you're upset that I'm leaving." Sarah sighs. "And... Look, I want to be honest with you. What's happened—it's changed everything for me. I'm sorry, Jemma, but it's only fair to tell you. I don't think I'm going to be coming back to work here."

Out of the corner of my eye I glimpse the dark shapes of her suitcases in the hall. She's already said goodbye to Finn, though I don't think he has any idea what's going on.

"It's not easy for me, and I know it must be very upsetting for you," Sarah continues, "especially after you rescued me so amazingly!"

"YES," I sniff.

"I want to explain. I want you to understand," she tells

me. "I haven't changed the way I feel about you. I still care about you. I still love you, Jemma."

"GET BETTER COME BACK," I sniff.

Sarah shakes her head. She looks like she's going to cry. "It's just that... What's happened, it's made me realize that I've been hiding here, in a way. This isn't actually my family, though I've kind of been pretending that it was."

She wipes a tear from her eye. "One day I'd like to have my own family and maybe be a foster parent like Lorraine. I think being here has been an excuse to not grow up, and what's happened these last few weeks has made me grow up—fast. Do you understand, Jemma?"

Of course I do. What she's saying does make sense. I've just been fighting it. I want her to stay so much. I don't reply.

"And maybe," she continues, "it's not so good for you to be so dependent on me. I know you need care, but other aides might be just as good or better—or different anyway, and give you different experiences."

I'd love to tell her about Rosie. I don't want other aides, even though Sheralyn's been okay. I want Sarah.

"I don't want to stop you growing up and experiencing new things. And this sniff controller—it's amazing! It's going to change your life completely. You will have so much more control."

I know she's right. You can't always keep things the same. I think about Jodi... New experiences can be good. I think about my future now I can communicate, all the possibilities. But...

"Tell me you understand. Please?"

Part of me wants to, but the rest of me refuses.

I know it's selfish, but I want her to stay.

She strokes my hand. She looks at the sniff-controller screen—but I am not sniffing.

Then she looks at me, and I see the pain in her face. She has been through so much. Suddenly, I see I am hurting her, and I don't want to do that.

"Please, Jemma?"

Sarah waits patiently while I sniff each letter. "YES," I sniff. "LOVE YOU SARAH."

Then as she hears the words spoken, she leans forward to hug me as best she can. I feel the wetness of her face as she kisses my cheek. I am crying too.

She lets go. Then she gets a tissue and gently wipes my eyes. "I'll keep in touch, Jemma, I promise. Your dad says you'll be able to text and email with this thing. It'll be great!"

She gives me her warmest smile and walks toward the door.

"BYE SARAH," I sniff.

And then she is gone.

55

Nine Months Later

I'm being pushed in my wheelchair, and I am surrounded by people. I have never seen so many people, and they all seem so tall and so close that I feel as if my chair and I are going to disappear under the crowd—flattened on the sidewalk. I'm trying not to be scared.

My new aide, Alice, is pushing me. I was anxious before she started, but I was surprised to find I actually liked her right away. I had wanted it to be just me and Jodi, but the good thing is that with Alice pushing me, Jodi can walk beside me. Now and then she squeezes my hand. I catch the glint of her midnight-blue nail polish and look with pleasure at my own matching nails. I think of Sarah—that day when she did my nails, the awful things that followed. It feels so long ago now.

I didn't realize it would be so far. We seem to go on and on. I'm glad it's not raining.

"I cannot *believe* we're really here!" says Jodi.

I've talked so much to Jodi. We meet up every weekend. Mom and Dad decided not to take a break from fostering, to my relief. They asked me if I'd like to go to Carlstone College in a few years, and I would. Mom's finding out about applying for a place, but I don't know if I'll get funding. In the meantime I've started going to a mainstream school for part of the week. I was really nervous, but Jodi encouraged me to try it. I wanted to go to her school, but the school district said a nearer one was more suitable. So I tried it—and I love it! It's not easy, but I have a teaching assistant to help me and everything is so interesting. At first I was going two days a week there, and now I'm going three.

I have new communication software, and I've had lots of training with a speech therapist who specializes in AAC. She's been amazing, and now I can select words and phrases from categories rather than spelling everything out. It's still very slow, but faster than typing each letter. I know it will take time, but I want to do my exams and go to college—just like Jodi plans to do.

I am also going on a sailing trip for teenagers with disabilities. Alice loves water sports, and she told me she used to help on sailing trips as a volunteer. I searched the internet using my sniff controller and found out more about it myself, and I've already been on a day's sailing class. It was amazing! Beats the local park any day.

And Olivia came home! Mom and Dad were eager to have her, and I told the social workers I wanted to give Olivia a chance too. It was weird how much I missed her in the weeks she was away. Her social worker has organized some therapy for her. She's a little quieter than she was, but not much, and she still has tantrums. She talks to me sometimes, though, and it's wonderful to be able to talk back. She's still going to ballet lessons too. Olivia never explained why she took the money. She said she didn't know and that she just wanted it.

Finn seemed happier when Olivia came back. He is doing better, though it's not always easy to tell with him. He hasn't done any head-banging for months, at least. Mom hopes one day he'll be able to communicate too.

I've had a few emails from Sarah. She's still living with her sister, and she says they're getting along really well. I miss her, but I'm glad—because I have my sister, and Sarah is with hers too. She finally broke up with Richard. I hope she'll find someone who will be right for her one day.

Next month is Dan's trial for kidnapping her. He's pleading not guilty, but the police have plenty of evidence against him. Dan and Billy's trial for Ryan's murder will be soon too. They may show my video in court. If they do, it will be the first time someone has given evidence using a sniff controller.

I suddenly realize we have arrived. This place is massive! Jodi is speaking to someone who's wearing a hat and looks like he works here. She's pointing to my wheelchair and asking which way to go.

We go up in an elevator. First stop is the accessible bathroom. Now we are back with Jodi and searching for the where we want to be. So many people!

Jodi leads the way through an entrance labeled Block C, and Alice pushes me quickly after her. We're at the front of a balcony in a wheelchair space with seats on either side. I can't believe how vast this place is. It's a huge oval shape, and I can see rows and rows of people below and across the other side who look as small as insects!

"You okay, Jemma?" Alice asks, moving around to face me.

"THIRSTY," I sniff. "DRINK."

Alice reads the words as they appear, and I don't bother to press the speaker. It is so noisy in here that I don't think she'd hear—even with the volume on full. "Of course," says Alice. She rummages in the bag for my drink and opens it. It's taken a while, but I'm getting used to being able to ask for what I want.

Once I've had a drink, Alice gently puts small earplugs in my ears. "NO!" I sniff. I am worried I won't hear well.

"You'll need them!" Alice tells me, and Jodi nods in agreement.

"Seriously, Jemma. It's *so* loud!" she warns me.

"EXCITING!" I sniff.

Jodi smiles back.

Then suddenly, there they are. They look so small on that

faraway stage, but the screens are big so I can see their faces clearly. Glowlight! It is really them. I see Leo! My heart thuds. He is gorgeous.

The music starts. It is like a musical thunderstorm.

The beat is so loud and the vibration so strong I can feel it in every bone of my body. Then the voices. It is so loud—so incredible. I sing along in my head. I catch a glimpse of Jodi's ecstatic face. She squeezes my hand.

I am here at a Glowlight concert with my sister. She is glowing.

I am alight!

AUTHOR'S NOTE

When I began to write this book, I had not decided how Jemma was going to be able to communicate, although I knew she would need to by the end! Advances in technology have made communication possible for many more people with disabilities. However, there are lots of people who do not have access to this technology or are unable to use it for various reasons.

The device that Jemma uses in the book is inspired by a real invention, developed by researchers at the Weizmann Institute in Israel. Trials have shown that some people with severe disabilities and people with locked-in syndrome, for whom other systems have not worked, have been able to use this device. And as a relatively inexpensive product, it has the potential to make AAC technology accessible for more people than ever before. It has not yet gone into production, but my hope is that by raising awareness, this book may help

persuade a company to take this up and make it commer-
cially available. I dream that one day everyone who has the
potential to communicate will have access to the equipment
they need.

A CONVERSATION WITH THE AUTHOR

What inspired you to write *I Have No Secrets*?

I enjoy reading thrillers myself, and I had this idea for a story in which the protagonist knows the identity of the killer but can't tell anyone for some reason. The character of Jemma sprung into my head. I think she came from my experience of volunteer work with people with disabilities. I was very shy as a child, and this led to an interest in people for whom communication is difficult for more physical reasons.

Why was it important to you to write a protagonist with cerebral palsy (CP)?

Although I set out to write a thriller, and the character with CP was secondary to this, once I'd decided on a character with CP, I realized how little representation there is in fiction. I wanted people with CP to see themselves in books and for other people to increase their awareness through reading. I also wanted to represent Jemma as an ordinary teenager who happens to have a disability.

CP affects people in different ways. What gave you the idea to make Jemma struggle to communicate with people as a key part of the plot?

Jemma's inability to tell anyone what she knew was central to the idea for the plot. I therefore needed her disability to be severe enough for her not to be able to communicate. I was, however, determined from the start that this would be more than a "plot ploy" and use it as an opportunity to explore Jemma's life and family relationships too.

What kind of research did you do to write this book?

It was vital to me to reflect Jemma's experiences as accurately and authentically as possible. I researched by talking to people—most importantly people with disabilities, including those with severe cerebral palsy and those with other disabilities but who use AAC (Augmentative and Alternative Communication). I also talked to relatives, caregivers, and other people who work with people with cerebral palsy.

I read books and researched online, and it was an online search that led me to a possible way for Jemma to communicate. Once I had a first draft, I got lots of feedback from people with direct experience and made changes accordingly. When one man with severe cerebral palsy said he thought his parents would understand better what it was like to be him through reading my book, I felt reassured that I was on the right path.

Why did you choose to write about a foster family?

When I was doing voluntary work, I met some wonderful foster parents who took in children with multiple and complex needs and disabilities. I thought a family like this would be a perfect setting for Jemma's story.

You've worked as a support teacher for children who are hearing impaired, as a reading recovery teacher, as an adult education teacher, and as a teacher of adults recovering from and experiencing mental health issues. What impact did those teaching experiences have on your writing?

I think my teaching experiences have helped me empathize with people who have all kinds of barriers to overcome in order to learn and in order to live life in the way they want. I recognize the frustrations and the need for people to listen, to have patience, to offer support, and to not be afraid to ask for and receive support. I think my writing is impacted by every person I meet, and I enjoy connecting with people as a teacher and hearing their stories too.

What were the easiest and hardest parts about writing *I Have No Secrets*?

The easiest part was Jemma's voice. Because she spoke so

clearly in my head and felt so alive, it was easy to write from her perspective. The hardest part was the writer's block that I experienced from time to time when I wasn't sure how to bridge the gap from one part of the plot to another. I sometimes didn't write anything for weeks.

What is your writing process like?

I am a plotter—I like to have the framework of the story worked out before I've gotten very far with it. I tend to write best first thing in the morning. I write mainly on a computer at home but sometimes write by hand in the garden or go to a library or café.

What did you edit *out* of this book?

I had written more about Sarah's relationship with her own sister, which was cut during the editing process.

What would you like readers to take away from the novel?

I mainly hope readers will have enjoyed the read, but I also hope they will feel more aware and more confident about interacting with people with disabilities.

I hope readers will see that life can have value even for someone who can't communicate, but that communication gives power and autonomy, and we should do everything we can to give people a voice and to listen to one another too.

READING GROUP GUIDE

1. Discuss the contrast between the way Dan speaks to Jemma and the way he speaks to everyone else. Why do you think he speaks to Jemma the way he does? Which voice do you think is the "true" Dan?

2. What makes Sarah a good caregiver for Jemma?

3. How did you feel toward Richard? Did you suspect he might be guilty? Did you hope that he would get together with Sarah in the end?

4. Finn, like Jemma, faces communication challenges. What role do you think he plays in the story?

5. Why do you think Olivia acts the way she does? How do you think her story might continue?

6. Can you imagine Jodi's expectations about meeting Jemma
    and why she reacts the way she does when they first meet?

7. When a passerby offers Jemma's caregiver money, why do
    you think Jemma feels so upset?

8. Has the book changed the way you feel about the life or
    experiences of someone who can't communicate or move
    independently?

9. Do you know anyone who has difficulty with communica-
    tion or uses alternative means of communication like sign
    language or AAC? Can you think of any ways in which
    you could support them more?

10. Have you ever felt burdened with someone else's secret
    and felt that you wanted to or needed to share the secret?

11. Sarah was two-timing Dan. Do you think she deserved
    what happened to her?

12. How do you think Jemma's life will be changed by the
    events of the story going forward?

13. Why do you think Jemma's foster parents decided to foster
    her and the other children?

14. Imagine Jemma's family going on vacation. What would they need to think about to ensure all needs are met and they have a good trip?

15. What was the most moving moment of the story for you?

ACKNOWLEDGMENTS

First, I would like to thank my lovely agent, Anne Clark. I couldn't ask for a better agent, and your commitment to this book has been wonderful. I am so lucky too to have brilliant editors in Stella Paskins and Liz Bankes at Egmont. Your skillful editing, enthusiasm, and excitement about the book have been amazing. Thank you to the whole team at Egmont! And thank you to the team at Sourcebooks, too, for all your work on the U.S. edition.

I am eternally grateful to all those people who took the time to answer my questions and to read the manuscript and give feedback at various stages. Any errors are my own and not the fault of anyone acknowledged here.

For help with cerebral palsy and AAC information, I am especially grateful to Jonathan Kaye, Ellie Simpson of CPTeens, and Debbie Simpson, Natasha Bello, Julie Bello, and Kate McCallum from 1Voice, Kate Caryer from Communication Matters and Unspoken Theatre, and Jenny

Herd from Communication Matters. Thanks also to Carl Ritchie, Joan Ritchie, and Kevin Robinson who answered police-related questions for me.

From the Weizmann Institute, I would like to thank Lee Sela and Noam Sobel for answering many questions about their recently developed communication device.

I would not be the writer I am without fabulous City Lit, where I started out as a student and now teach. From there, I formed my own Friday writing workshop, with talented writers Jo Barnes, Angela Kanter, Vivien Boyes, and Derek Rhodes. Your constructive criticism and support have meant so much to me. I'd also like to thank my young adult beta readers, including those found for me by Janis Inwood, librarians at Southgate School, where I was educated, and Jessica Pliskin, whose excellent suggestion really helped.

My family—every one of you, I thank you for your support—and especially my husband, Adam, for all his love and for putting up with my mind being elsewhere a lot of the time (and for his helpful suggestion, gratefully received and ignored, that I should write about zombies). Final thanks go to our children, Michael and Zoe, to whom this book is dedicated. I know you are annoyed at not being old enough to read it yet—but you will be, one day, and I enjoy watching you grow so, so much.

ABOUT THE AUTHOR

Penny Joelson was born in London, where she still lives with her husband and two children and teaches creative writing. She began working with people with disabilities when she was a teenager, which gave her the inspiration and insight for *I Have No Secrets*. Find Penny on Twitter @pennyjoelson.

FIREreads

❂ #getbooklit

Your hub for the hottest young adult books!

Visit us online and sign up for our
newsletter at FIREreads.com

 @sourcebooksfire

 sourcebooksfire

 firereads.tumblr.com